Melancholy Magic

A BRYLIE SCOTT PARACOZY MYSTERY

MILLIE THORNE

kinship press

To all of those forced to carry the weight of grief

EBook: 978-1-954702-34-9
Paperback: 978-1-954702-35-6
Hardcover: 978-1-954702-43-1
Large Print Hardcover: 978-1-954702-36-3

Edited by Lisa Hollett, Silently Correcting Your Grammar, LLC
Cover by Jacqueline Sweet
For inquiries, contact authormilliethorne@gmail.com

Welcome to Reverie Springs...

DON'T MIND THE HEXES

millie
THORNE

Chapter One

Fresh starts were *not* supposed to smell like dead fish.

"Now, Brylie, I know the store needs some cleaning up." The woman I'd just met—the one with the impossible name of Gwendolyn—practically paraded through the darkened store, flipping switches and attempting to brighten the space with overly harsh fluorescent lighting. "My friend Rose made a good go of this place, but it was her dream and not mine. I didn't even know what to do with all this stuff when she passed. So now, it's yours. A brand-new dream come to life."

Because I totally had dreams of running a hardware store in a town with a smaller population than my high school graduating class. The fish smell? Definitely dreamy.

I jumped as a creature—whether a huge spider, a small mouse, or some sort of freakish hybrid was too hard to tell—scampered under one of the shelving fixtures. Living the dream, all right.

Note to self: buy something to shoot flames at unwanted guests.

"I think there may have been some mistake," I said, feeling very much like Dorothy in Oz finding out the wizard was really just a self-important old man who couldn't get her home...but without the cool shoes. "I thought you said this was a successful local hardware store."

Like the one I'd run with my dad for nearly fifteen years. Like the one I'd been forced to leave behind when he'd died with a mountain of debt hanging over his head. Like the one she'd promised me on the phone when she'd said I should move all the way across the country to Reverie Springs because she was some long-lost relative and I was the great-niece whom she wanted to inherit the family business.

Successful did not mean layers of dust and a space that smelled so foul, I practically had to hold my breath.

"This *was* a successful hardware store, Brylie. Rose was a great businesswoman and did well here, but as I said—this wasn't my dream. I know nothing about the business side of things, so I shut the doors and figured I'd wait to find you. My only family." Gwendolyn gave me a slow smile, clasping her hands in front of her. "And here you are."

"Here I am, all right." I sighed, looking around at too many months—maybe years—of neglect and calculating ways to fix what was wrong. Starting with the smell. The stench hung heavy in the air. Enough so that I worried about my dog's health. Thankfully Elmer, my right-hand Basset hound and literal best friend, didn't seem bothered. In fact, as soon as I stopped walking, he whined and huffed, plopping down right there in the middle of the main aisle. And then he started to snore.

Gwendolyn frowned at the pile of bone and fur and chub. "Your dog seems awfully tired."

Understatement. "Yeah, he's taking aging really hard."

"How old is he?"

"Two." Leaving the laziest dog on earth to his nap, I continued deeper into the store. If Elmer ended up at the mercy of some sort of spider-mouse demon creature, that was on him. I had a business to figure out, and I was much better at back-end stuff than front-end. Customer service had been my dad's realm. I'd learn it, but not today. I needed to deep-dive the actual business setup. "Do you have any records from when the store was open? Any sort of distributor listings or wholesaler contacts?"

Gwendolyn nodded, her white-and-silver braid bouncing and an almost annoying sense of lightness around her, as if she'd never been happier than right in that moment. With me. In the abandoned, stinky store.

"I'm sure Rose had something like that. I kept everything the way she left it—I never even touched her files."

Files. That word made me think of paper, which sent a shot of something like unease straight into my belly. *Please be wrong.* "Did she leave her computer here in the store, too?"

"Rose? She didn't use a computer, dear."

Okay, so...paper records. I'd need to spend a little time figuring that out, for sure. I couldn't even remember a time when we'd used paper records. "And the smell? Do you have any idea what that might be?"

"Oh, that's my fault. It's hexing day, so I'm brewing a potion."

I stopped hard enough to rattle my brain and performed a slow turn that would have fit perfectly in a horror movie. "Excuse me?"

"Hexing day, dear. It's today." Gwendolyn smiled, the wrinkles around her eyes growing deeper with the movement, as if she were talking about spaghetti Wednesday or taco Tuesday.

"Potions?" Because I still couldn't believe my ears.

Gwendolyn didn't even falter, though. "Yes. I take all the negativity people have tossed my way, brew a strong potion filled with healing intentions, and then go around town spraying it on those who caused me vexation."

"You...hex people."

"Yes."

"Every week."

"Good heavens, no. That would be excessive." She laughed, as if normal people talked about their hexing schedule all the time. Perhaps they did in Reverie Springs—I really had no point of reference to go off.

"How often do you...hex people?" The words didn't quite roll off the tongue. No siree Bob.

"The best time to brew this sort of potion is at the new moon, so I only hex people once a month."

Sure. That was *much* better than weekly hexing. "Well, I guess if that's the best time for such things."

"Certainly. You can't let negativity fester, dear."

She met my gaze, her light eyes locking on mine, and for a moment—a brief second of time—I felt something that stole my breath. Sadness. Every bit of light I'd noticed earlier vanished, the happiness extinguished. Instead, I felt so much true and honest sorrow hidden away inside her. The sort of sharp, painful emotion that weighs you down and dulls your entire existence. Everything stopped as the gravity of the moment pulled me into an abyss of someone else's making, as the pressure of the fall sucked me deeper and deeper into the pain that could only be coming from her.

And then, without a word, Gwendolyn looked away,

breaking the connection and locking those feelings inside herself. I gasped, sucking in oxygen as if I'd been drowning, reaching to hold myself upright as the world began to spin again. As my heart slowed to a more normal rhythm.

Ignore, ignore, ignore. It's nothing. Nothing at all.

I coughed once, trying hard to hide the way my hands shook. Hoping against hope that she couldn't see how much that look had affected me.

She had, of course. "Are you all right, dear?"

"I'm fine," I replied, taking a few extra seconds to compose myself before pushing off the shelf and heading toward the back where the office had to be. Shoving everything I'd just experienced down into a pit where I could ignore it. Just as I'd been taught to do. "So...your friend Rose ran the store?"

Fake it till you make it was a way of life, after all.

We continued through the sad little retail space, Gwendolyn chattering on about spells and tinctures and customers who used to come into the store as I did my best to ignore the remnants of sadness licking at my skin. If I didn't, I might become more invested in her emotional state. Might try to work out why she radiated pain. *Not your problem, your business, or anything to talk about,* my dad had always said when I'd brought up how I sometimes felt other people's emotions. I tried to stick to that advice and ignore the pull to involve myself in their drama, but there were times when that seemed impossible. Like the moment with Gwendolyn. That sadness hadn't been weak or new—the feeling had carried a physical weight, had felt old and solid. The sort of emotional trauma that Gwendolyn wouldn't—or couldn't—let go of. I was just nosy enough to want to know why but not motivated enough to actually ask.

Besides, I had my own issues to worry about. Starting

with the sight before me as we turned into a little room at the back of the storage area. "These are Rose's...business files?"

"Yes, dear. All right where she left them."

And where she'd left them was piled high on every flat surface of what might have been called an office. There were no filing cabinets, only files. Boxes and boxes of paper tucked inside manila folders and stacked haphazardly around the room. It would likely take me a week just to clear off one desk —and there were two of them—plus more time to audit the towers on the floor and the windowsill and...

"This is too much," I said, frozen in the doorway. Unable to look away from the train wreck before me. "I don't even know where to start."

"You start wherever the spirit tells you to," Gwendolyn said, nodding toward the mountain of paper before me. "Go ahead. Feel where to go."

Looking at the stacks of paper, the only place I felt like going was out the door and back to California. But I had nothing left there; my dad was dead, his store sold off to a competitor, and his house taken by the bank. I'd never known my mother—creator of the great-aunt Gwendolyn connection —and I had no other family that I knew of. My entire world had come crashing down right before my thirtieth birthday, so this was it. Reverie Springs and I needed to get along until I figured out where to go next.

But that didn't mean I needed to play into the hands of a woman claiming to be some sort of witch. It also meant the paperwork could wait. It wasn't like those stacks were going anywhere.

"I think where I feel the need to go is to lunch." I kept my eyes locked on Gwendolyn's ear—not wanting to meet that pained gaze again any time soon—and gave her the best smile I could. "Is there any place to eat around here?"

Gwendolyn frowned, those hands once more clasped before her. "Of course. There's a diner right next door. It's very popular for breakfast and lunch, though only open for dinner on the weekends."

A breakfast and lunch joint. I loved it. "Perfect. Why don't you join me? My treat."

I hurried from the claustrophobia-inducing office and through the store, noting the outdated product selection and dust-covered packaging along the way. Fighting the tightening between my shoulder blades, I began calculating the amount of work needed to bring this place up to my standards. A lot—it would be *a lot* of work. Weeks if not months of hard-core research and physical labor. More than I'd been prepared for.

When Gwendolyn had reached out to me after my dad's death to say she had a house and a business for me if I was willing to come to Reverie Springs, I'd been skeptical. Things like that—long-lost relatives and secret inheritances—didn't happen in the real world. Still, I'd been at a strange crossroads in my life. Realizing you had nothing of substance and no real opportunities in the place you'd always lived left you a bit more adventurous than normal. Instead of ignoring the supposed windfall, I'd packed up what little I had left after the bill collectors and estate sales, tossed Elmer's lazy butt in the front seat of my minivan, and driven east to a place I'd never heard of, let alone visited. Reverie Springs, Vermont. Home of the Reverie Springs Hardware store, which I now owned. Also home to Willow Manor, which I also apparently owned. And, completing the trifecta, home to my dead mother, whom I'd never met.

What had I been thinking?

I followed Gwendolyn next door, leaving a barely awake Elmer on the sidewalk by the entrance to the diner with a firm *stay* command. Not that he needed one—the dog let out a rumbling snore before I even made it inside.

Gwendolyn led me into the diner and to a table of dark wood surrounded by four heavy black chairs. Mercury glass mirrors reflected the sunlight around the small space and kept it from seeming too dark, but that was about it in the way of decoration. Masculine—that was the only word I could think of to describe the decor and vibe of the place. Not a single feminine touch in the room, and yet it felt cozy and calm. Lovely, really.

"So," Gwendolyn said once she had her napkin placed in her lap, garnering my attention. "Tell me more about California. I've always been so curious about the West Coast."

"You've never been?"

"No. I've spent most of my life right here in Reverie Springs."

Quaint, and not at all surprising. "And my mom was born here."

"Oh, yes. Such a tiny little thing, my sweet Carolyn. She had these huge, dark eyes that seemed to devour the world around her...very much like yours." Her expression turned softer, her smile a little sadder. "I can see so much of her in you."

I couldn't help it—I had to look. Had to get a little taste of what she felt. So I did, and the old woman stared right back as if she knew what I was doing. As if she understood the unexplainable desire to let go and just *feel*.

And maybe she did, because as she held my gaze, something thumped inside me. Some sort of ache or pain or twinge. Something that spoke of years of wanting to know someone I'd lost. Of an obsession I'd tucked away many, many moons before. Almost as if she were somehow reflecting my own emotions instead of showing me hers. No one had ever done that to me before.

I didn't like it.

I dropped my gaze to the wood tabletop, breaking the connection. "My dad used to say he could see lifetimes in my mom's eyes."

"That's not surprising. She had beautiful eyes." Gwendolyn reached across the table and patted my hand. "I'm so sorry you lost her as young as you did. It would have been a gift to get to know her."

I looked up, locking eyes again. Seeking that connection, curious for it. *Sadness, but different this time. Deeper and even older. A dull ache instead of a sharp stab.* Still a sense of something lost, though.

I understood loss all too well.

I broke the stare, not wanting to feel her emotions any longer, not needing to delve that deep into things that would just remind me of my dad's death. But taking my gaze away from Gwendolyn brought my eyes to the man behind the counter. The one looking my way with an actual landline phone handset pressed against his ear. The one who was tall and thick with wild dark hair and an air of malice. He wore a white chef's jacket, sported a bushy beard, and had a serious frown on his face as he spoke into the antiquated device that was attached to the wall via those curly cords my old store had occasionally sold. Our eyes met for the briefest of moments as he moved to hang up the phone, but that was all it took to know he was in a bad mood. Why, I had no idea—not my circus, not my monkeys—but he made me uncomfortable enough to want to leave with that one single second of connection. I would have done just that, but the waitress showed up before I could rise from my chair.

A waitress Gwendolyn apparently knew. "Hi, Mary. We'll both have the soup of the day and a salad. Do you like salad, Brylie?" Gwendolyn looked at me with those big pale-green eyes of hers. Expectant. Excited. About lettuce.

"Yeah. Salad sounds great."

I ran my blunt nails over the inside of my wrist and waited for the waitress to leave before bringing up the next item on my Reverie Springs to-do list. "You said on the phone that there's a house I'm inheriting as well, right?"

Gwendolyn raised her glass to her lips, frowning slightly before taking a sip. Delaying her answer just long enough to make me begin to feel a bit of trepidation.

Now what?

"Yes. Willow Manor," she finally said, her voice a little darker. "It's technically my house, but I have no need for something so large. It's a much better fit for someone younger, like you."

"Where do you live?"

"Over the hardware store, of course."

Of course. "And the monthly hexing potions…"

"The customers won't complain about the smell, dear," she said as if reading my mind. Or perhaps noticing the way I scrunched my nose at the memory of the stench. "They never have before."

Or they wouldn't come in on hexing days. I'd need to figure out how to work that particular monthly dip into my sales plans.

The food came quickly enough and was surprisingly good. Even the salad, while still only a salad, was fresh and crisp and very filling with these amazingly sweet little nut things that I couldn't stop eating. I would have given my compliments to the chef—not really, because no one actually did that, especially not in a diner—but the angry man behind the counter didn't seem like the type you paid a compliment to.

"Do you hex him?" I asked, nodding toward the man in question.

"Ander?" She shook her head, that silver-gray braid moving right along with her. "Oh no, dear. He's one of the nicest men in town. I would never."

Nice? I risked another peek, nearly cowering under the weight of his frown, cringing as he slammed a pan onto the stove as if it had somehow offended him. If he was one of the nicest, I'd hate to meet the rest of the men. Which could be a problem, seeing as how I sort of liked men. In a purely dating sort of way. I might never date again if *that* was what was considered nice around these parts, though.

"Here," Gwendolyn said, pulling me from my thoughts of evil men torturing the women of this town as she set a pair of keys on the table. "One for the store and one for Willow Manor. They're all yours."

Mine. I'd never had anything that was actually mine other than my car and Elmer. Though the dog would probably argue that I was *his* human and not the other way around. He'd be right, too. So basically, my sole possessions were a fifteen-year-old minivan, a store that smelled like rotting fish guts, and an old house.

Seemed positive.

"You should get out to the manor soon," Gwendolyn said, waving for the waitress—Mary—to come back. "I'd hate for you to drive out there in the dark on your first trip. The gardens are still so beautiful."

"You're not coming with me?"

"No, dear. I have a few things to do this afternoon."

Something close to an irritation danced upon my skin, a sensation of itchiness making me far too aware of my body. A feeling I knew all too well. Great-Aunt Gwendolyn wasn't telling the truth for some reason. My intuition never lied... unlike the people around me. I didn't call her on her little fib, though. There was no reason to. It seemed like a harmless sort of untruth.

Gwendolyn glanced up as the waitress approached then slipped her some money before I could say anything. Mary smiled and retreated, shrugging as if this was a normal Gwendolyn thing. And perhaps it was. The women of Reverie Springs were plotting against me, it seemed.

"I offered to take you," I said, trying not to sound too harsh. "You turned me into a liar."

But Gwendolyn just laughed and shook her head. "Not a liar, dear. I'll let you pay next time."

Her words brought about another need to scratch at my arms—another little white lie.

"No, you won't."

She grinned my way. "Probably not. Now, quit quibbling with me about such trivial things. You go and see the manor. I had the utilities turned back on when you said you'd be willing to come to Reverie Springs, so you should have everything you need there."

Except someone who knew where the place was and why it was being handed over to me. "Okay, well... Thanks so much for lunch."

"My pleasure." She gripped my hand while staring straight into my eyes, dropping all her sadness into my lap in a way that felt intentional. Leaning closer as I gasped for air and began to shake. "You are a talented one, aren't you?"

I wasn't able to take a breath big enough to answer her, so I didn't. Couldn't. Instead, I stayed rooted to the spot as she took a good look at me, only taking control of my body back when she finally dropped her gaze to the table.

"What did you do?" I asked, my voice harsh and soft.

Gwendolyn smiled, the look doing nothing to remove the sorrow from her expression. "Nothing, dear. I just wanted to see it for myself."

"Well, don't do it again. Ever." I rose from my chair, stumbling for the door and rushing outside. Air. I needed air.

Elmer jumped up when I burst through the door, growling low as if he could stave off the storm of emotions—other people's, not mine—to protect me. My brave boy. I knelt next to him for a solid minute or two, stroking the soft fur of his ears and collecting myself. Releasing all the pain that had been shoved at me and reclaiming the calm I strove for. The state of an almost-emotionless existence I worked hard to maintain. But then I got really mad at my great-aunt Gwendolyn, which totally blew up the idea of calm or emotionless.

Crazy old lady.

But anger never got anyone anywhere, and I didn't brew hexing potions on the new moon to smite those who'd caused me vexation. So instead, I took a few deep breaths to regain control of my temper, and I patted my dog on the head.

"Elmer, I think we've found ourselves in some sort of alternate universe. One I'm not sure we're ready for."

The Basset hound yawned and flopped over to lay his head against the side of my thigh. There may have been a tail wag in there—just one. Never let it be said that my dog was anything other than lazy. I blew out a breath, took a moment to shake off the tingle of dread teasing the back of my skull, rose to my feet, and headed for my car. Ready to drive out of town and find Willow Manor. My new home.

"Excuse me," a middle-aged lady said as soon as I opened the passenger door to let Elmer inside the van. "He can't run around like that."

Considering the dog had promptly taken a seat on the sidewalk the second we'd stopped walking, I wasn't sure what *him* the woman was talking about.

"You mean my dog?"

"Yes," she said, frowning at Elmer. "There are leash laws in Reverie Springs."

Of course there were. "He doesn't need a leash."

"Every dog needs a leash."

Elmer sighed and lay on the cement, not even bothering to pretend to stay awake. My goodness, his snoring was getting worse.

"He doesn't need a leash. He barely needs oxygen." Still, I bent down and picked up Elmer the best I could, pushing him into the passenger seat of my van. "Besides, we're leaving."

The woman—all five-foot-five of her with one of those haircuts that screamed "I want to speak to a manager"—huffed and scrunched her nose. "Fine. But he still needs a leash."

I caught what I thought was a whisper of alcohol on her breath, which normally I wouldn't have given a second thought to—not my business and all—except that it was awfully early in the day to be hitting the bottle and she seemed a little uptight to be the cocktails-over-lunch type. Something didn't fit, but I wasn't in the mood to delve into it. Besides, it was time to check out my new home.

"What my dog needs is a nap, but thanks for the advice." With that, I slammed the door and jogged around the front to the driver's side, ready to get the heck out of town. To run away from other people and hide for a few hours, just me and Elmer.

I slid into the van and fastened my seat belt, reaching across the console to clip Elmer to his as well. Safety first, and all. "C'mon, Elmer. Let's go check out our new home."

A new home. A house all to ourselves. It had to be better than the decaying old hardware store. It *had* to be.

Chapter Two

From death and decay to melancholy and desolation. There was no other way to describe the sensation chilling me to my bones as I stood on the porch of Willow Manor. The house, the air, the ground itself—they all gave off a definite sense of abandonment. Of the wretchedness that follows being left behind. I was quite familiar with the sensations, having buried my father all alone the month before. The sensation squelched my excitement and left me shivering in the early summer heat.

But I only had one option left after losing everything. So, I sighed, and I turned the key in the antique doorknob.

"Welcome home, Elmer." I stepped inside, sloshing through the foyer, distracted by every drip and growing more anxious as my socks became soaked inside my shoes. Water was everywhere. Lots of it. Covering the wood floors and inching up the tall baseboards, soaking into the rugs and dripping down the walls. The house was a virtual swamp. Great-Aunt Gwendolyn had definitely turned on the utilities. "We know the water works."

My soft murmur elicited nothing more than an irritated huff, as if even the dog didn't want to be there. I couldn't blame him—the house was not exactly ready for guests. Unless they were of the duck variety.

The emotional side of me wanted to run away from the pain this place telegraphed, but the rational side—the daughter of a hardware store owner side—knew a water leak was likely nothing more than a busted pipe. Fixable and completely normal, especially for older homes such as the manor. I could dig my toolbox out of the van and find the leak. I'd done similar repairs before.

I couldn't leave the house, though. Couldn't stand to abandon her, not even just to run to my car. Walls and floors and fixtures shouldn't emote, but the ones in the manor did. They *felt* something and were sure to make me aware of it. These rooms were downright lonely. The compulsion to stay, along with the desire to explore the space and take in the damage, ended up too tempting to resist. We walked deeper into the house, every footfall bringing out a creak or groan from the structure.

Antique pictures hung on walls, the ornate frames standing in stark contrast to the patterned paper behind them. Older faces stared back at me from within their dark outlines, stern and unforgiving in the moment they'd been captured. Hard eyes and stiff lips seemed to be the theme of the pictures. Not a single smile to be found in Willow Manor.

Farther into the house—down a hallway that led to a set of French doors so dirty, I could hardly see through them—the wallpaper had begun to fall, curling over the frames as if the wooden ovals and rectangles were all that lay between the strips of paper and the floor. Every section showed its creamy white backing, bent to the will of time and gravity. Other parts held firm, clinging to the plaster walls with something close to desperation. Those were the sections that seemed to be missing something, though. That bore the scars of whatever pictures had once hung on them. I could see where they'd been, could trace the shadows and shapes of the missing frames on the patterns below. How strange that the paper fell only from the parts where frames remained—as if the house had somehow hung on to the rest to hold it in place. As if wood and plaster had become cognizant enough to spread their tenacity to one and not the other.

"I'm anthropomorphizing a house, Elmer. I think that might be a sign of something wrong with me." As was talking to a dog like a human, but I chose to ignore that particular fact.

The long hallway bisected the house straight down the middle, giving me a path to follow. Doors sat half open, partially blocking my view into other rooms, looking incomplete in their motions. As if they ached to be either all the way open or fully closed, not lost somewhere in the limbo between.

And the paper. Pieces of it were everywhere. Scattered files and sheets of white decorated the dark wood floor with bright spots that sometimes crawled up the walls, adding strange islands of light in the sea of near-black beneath my feet.

But the worst had to be the water. It almost seemed to seep from within the structure itself, staining the ceiling and darkening the walls. Dripping and collecting on those beautiful wood floors. I couldn't stand the thought of so much water battling against a house. The liquid had a tendency to ruin what it touched. Basements, kitchens, lives...all manner of things could be destroyed if you added enough water.

"Maybe there's still a linen closet. I can grab the wet-dry vac from the van, and we could have this cleaned up in..." Yeah, no way could I say no time. The place was big, old, soaking wet...and, apparently, all mine.

Which meant it was my job to fix the problems within.

"Dad always said you could rule the world with the right toolbox." I glanced down at Elmer, but he had no comment. Not even a huff. He wasn't lying in the water snoring, though, so I considered that a win.

With a determination to repair what I could and a whispered promise to be right back, I headed outside to my van and opened the hatch. My tools sat in boxes on the right, and my handy wet-dry vac took up space on the left. I dragged everything onto the porch, dug through the boxes for what I needed, then walked back inside—wrench in hand and headlamp flashlight illuminated.

"Let's vanquish some plumbing problems, Elmer."

He did *not* seem enthused, choosing to hang out on the porch instead of braving the mess inside with me. Not that I could blame him.

Three hours later, I'd identified one leaky pipe with a fixable issue I could handle immediately, one I needed more supplies for, and had walked away from my inspection with an overall sense of confusion.

"Where is all this coming from?" I tossed another blanket over the foyer floor, trying once again to soak up the never-ending flood. "I've turned off the main water supply, but it's still dripping. This is insane. It's as if someone keeps coming behind me and turning on the taps."

Elmer didn't answer, though he did growl. Deeply. I almost took the noise to be his usual snore, but the rumble of it didn't fit. My dog wasn't usually that vocal, so I turned around to see what had bothered him. The dog sat staring at the entrance to the house, his floppy ears lifted and the hair on his neck standing on end. I followed his gaze—reluctantly, I might add —and spotted someone looking through the window beside the front door. A male someone.

Of course, I did what any thirty-year-old woman alone in a strange place would do when they spotted a man peeking at them through a window. I screamed.

The man—older with white hair, a blue collared shirt, and some seriously faded jeans...immediately noted and stored away in case any sort of legal authority needed to be informed— disappeared then came back, this time through the unlocked front door.

Smart, Brylie. Real smart.

"Who are you?" I yelled, holding my wrench over my head, ready to use it as a weapon.

He definitely didn't seem afraid of me and my hand tools. In fact, the only emotion I picked up from him was anger, and it was directed at me. "I should be asking you that. This isn't your house."

"Yes, it is."

"No, it's not. It's Miss Gwen's house."

Miss Gwen. As in Great-Aunt Gwendolyn. "I'm her niece, and she gave me this house."

He frowned, looking me up and down. "She gave you a house?"

"And a business. Neither of which has anything to do with you. Why are you here?"

"I keep an eye on the manor for Miss Gwen. I'm Carl, and I live next door."

"Oh." I lowered my wrench slowly, still unsure. Still ready to whack neighbor Carl if he came too close. "Well, I'm living here now."

"Living?" He looked around, his face contorting as he took

in the mess. "This place has been empty since Miss Rose passed away."

Not surprising, though Gwendolyn hadn't shared much about the loss of her friend. "How long ago was that?"

"Going on five years now."

Five years—the house, the store both abandoned and left to rot for five long years. And Gwendolyn...what? Sitting in her apartment over the closed store, brewing hex potions? That made no sense.

Know what else didn't make sense? Standing in my wet foyer with a strange man. "Well, I'm here now and will be bringing this house back to rights." As soon as I figured out how to do that. "There's no problem here."

He surveyed the room—the wallpaper half hanging from some walls, the water covering the floor, the blankets and towels scattered about trying to absorb the latter—and his frown deepened. "You might want to clean up this water."

"I'm trying to."

He caught my eye, and a feeling of intense worry shot through me like a bullet. He must have really liked this house at one time.

"Did you check the bathroom on this level? Looks like you might have a leak."

My eyebrow twitched, and the part of me that grew up with older men assuming I didn't know what I was doing swelled. "Yup. I checked. And the bathrooms on the second floor, and the kitchen, and the main line running into the house. So far, no luck."

"Might be from the third-floor bathroom."

There was a third floor? I couldn't even remember seeing stairs. Not that I'd tell him that. "There's no water on the second floor, so anything coming from the third would be unlikely."

"Huh," he said, obviously stumped. "Wish I would have known you were coming—I could have stopped by to check on the place. Since no one's been in here in so long and all."

My arm began to itch, but my usual response to a lie didn't seem likely. The house *had* been empty—that much was obvious. The itch had to be from something else. If there was some sort of creepy-crawly bacteria in the house, I was going to turn around and head straight back to California.

"I didn't know I would need someone to check on the place."

"Pity." Carl rubbed his toe against an obviously warped board sitting under half an inch of water. "These floors used to be nice."

"Yeah, well...now, they're garbage." Inexplicably, a creak issued from behind me, making me jump, and the drips increased in volume and tempo. I watched—unable to comprehend exactly what I was seeing—as a puddle formed in the middle of the sheet I'd just thrown down.

"Oh, shoot."

"You'll definitely have your hands full here," Carl said as he backed out the door. "I live just up the road a piece. You let me know if there's anything I can do for you."

"Yeah. Thanks." I took a breath, blowing it out through my nose as I surveyed my new domain. "This place is such a dump."

A deep moan echoed through the house, a noise that could have been the structure settling or a cavalcade of ghosts crying out their dissatisfaction at the fact that I was unable to stop the water from running all over the floor. It could really go either way.

"C'mon, old man," I said to Elmer as I grabbed my stuff and headed for the door. "Let's go pick up what we need to fix that other pipe. Maybe that's the reason this place is leaking like a sieve."

Likely not, but there wasn't much else I could do other than turn off the water at the main. Which I'd already done. And the leaking hadn't stopped. Still, I needed to replace the corroded valve I'd found. If that didn't work, I'd have to open up a wall or two and fix what I could. Either option included major cleanup before mold set in and repairs to ancient plaster walls. That meant a bigger mess and possibly more work than I was capable of doing myself.

Looked like Elmer and I were going to need some tools... and likely a different place to sleep.

Chapter Three

Main Street sat empty, the lights glowing from deep within the tall maple trees lining the road and casting shadows along the deserted sidewalks. If I'd somehow found myself in some sort of horror film, I would have been concerned that a treacherous creature would jump out of the darkness and whisk me away.

I was not in a movie, but I still quickened my steps to the front door of the hardware store. No sense charming the devil, and all that.

Elmer followed me inside, trotting off in the direction of the checkout counters as soon as I closed the door behind him. That reminded me of my dad's store and how Elmer had come to work with me every day, spending the hours napping behind the cash register stand or under my desk in the back. While that store and this one were of the same type—small, local hardware store—they were worlds apart. My dad's store had been spotless, well lit, and rarely empty. This place...it reeked of loneliness. Of abandonment.

Between the house and the store, my mood had rolled

straight into the land of hopelessness. This change, this move, may not have been the best idea. I hopped onto the register counter and looked out over the store, letting the feelings around me settle deeper.

So much sadness.

I'd felt the same at home, though. Had nearly choked on the sorrow radiating off the store the first day I'd walked in after my dad had died. When Gwendolyn had called me that night—merely one month after the death of the man who I'd thought was my only family—I'd assumed this whole Reverie Springs thing had been fated. Meant to be.

I was beginning to think it had been a coincidence that I should have ignored instead.

"Fresh start, right, Elmer? That's what we'd wanted."

He snorted in response, likely still smelling the hexes I no longer noticed. Whether they'd faded or I'd grown immune I had no idea. Didn't really matter, though. The memory of the stench had scared my olfactory organs forever.

"Right. Not so fresh after all." I slid off the counter and headed for the plumbing repair aisle, hoping against hope that the valve I needed to fix the leak I'd found at the manor would still be on the shelf. I didn't run into any spider-mice this time, but that wasn't to say they weren't waiting to jump out at me from every corner. Hence why I took a detour to the hardware section to grab an acetylene torch. I'd noted that I needed something to shoot flames at unwanted guests—the torch would certainly do the job.

A handful of minutes, a few jumps and squeaks as shadows crept a little too close for comfort, and a good Basset hound snoring session later, I had what I needed. I led Elmer outside, pausing only long enough to lock the door behind me. A light shone from the apartment over the store—Gwendolyn. Was she up there all alone? Planning out this week's hex recipients?

"Hexes. As in witches. Elmer, I am losing my hold on reality."

Witches weren't a thing. Magic didn't exist. And the feelings of sadness and loss that overwhelmed me in Reverie Springs? All in my head.

Except it wasn't just Reverie Springs. Those sensations had always been there. Other people's joy, their deceit, their pain... I'd felt them since I could remember. I'd assumed as a child that everyone did, but my dad had gotten concerned when I'd talked about the weight of grief on a neighbor after he'd lost his wife. He'd told me to push those feelings away, that life was hard enough with your own emotions, and that no one could feel the pain of someone else.

So, I'd done as he'd said. For over twenty years, I'd ignored the sensations of other peoples' feelings and focused on my own. I'd denied the fact that I *could* feel those things and kept my mind on how I *shouldn't*. But now... How could I deny anything anymore?

And how could I move to a town where the things that weren't real seemed to be glowing like a beacon in the dark? Maybe Reverie Springs wasn't meant to be my fresh start after all. Maybe it would soon be time to move on to a new place. One without so much turmoil.

Which was something that required a lot of thought and focus, things I did not have the time for.

"Come on, Elmer. Let's go home." My four-legged bestie followed me to the van, dragging himself into the front seat as if those couple of inches he had to climb were too hard to complete. And yet, I couldn't blame him for his lack of energy.

Elmer was definitely tired, as was I. We both needed a place to sleep and a few hours of solid unconsciousness.

But when I pulled up to Willow Manor, the dread that I'd experienced earlier—the heartbreaking heaviness of the place—struck me once more, and I knew there was no way I could step in there. The very idea of walking through those doors made my throat tighten and my heart pound heavy in my chest.

Not tonight.

I stayed in my car instead, giving the manor a good long look. Seeking something that would explain why the place made me feel so sad. The house sat bathed in moonlight, the walls practically glowing. The dark shutters flanking the windows seemed to be eating the shadows for dinner, and the trees made light and dark dance together across the roof without music. The night, though, was anything but silent. Insects and critters I doubted I could identify filled the humid air with sounds the likes of which I hadn't experienced in California. Thick, melodic buzzing set the background noise, caws and hoots making themselves heard at various points.

So magical.

Everything about the house and the place held such beauty, such a sense of lost comfort and enchantment, but I couldn't go inside. Couldn't stand to look at all the damage and things that needed to be repaired. The things I didn't know if I could do. I was a handy girl, but this might have been too much for me. Add in the sensation of drowning every time I walked in the door, and there was no way I was going back in tonight. Which left me with few options.

I didn't know where a hotel might be and didn't want to sleep in the hardware store, so I did the only thing I could. I moved the car to the side of the house so people on the road wouldn't notice it, locked the doors, cracked the windows just enough to get a little air, curled up in the back seat with Elmer, and fell asleep right there in my van parked in the shadows of the manor.

One night outside wouldn't kill me.

I woke with a start what felt like minutes later. The early morning sun was just beginning to shine down on the van, making the inside way too hot to be comfortable. Sweat dripped down my forehead and neck, and the sense of not being able to breathe felt far more real than what I had experienced inside the house. Likely what had woken me. That or Elmer's deep, booming bark. He may have been lazy, but he was still good for some things—like keeping the two of us from roasting in my van.

I threw open the doors and practically fell outside, Elmer following right behind me with an energetic bark. One that definitely seemed out of place. Or maybe he was really happy that I'd finally woken up and gotten us out of that sweatbox.

Yeah, probably the second option.

"I guess we should get up and start the day, huh, Elmer?" I stood and brushed the grass from my legs while keeping an eye on the house. I still sensed a sadness there, but the fear from last night—the dread—didn't run as deep. Didn't stop me from wanting to finish what I'd started. Perhaps my newfound positivity came from the fact that sunlight filled the world or that I'd gotten some decent rest, but whatever it was, I no longer felt afraid at the idea of walking inside the place. Which meant it was time to get to work. "C'mon, boy. Let's go see if we can fix that leak. A shower would probably be a good idea after all the sweating in the van."

He sniffed my ankle and huffed, totally unimpressed.

Once I grabbed my keys and the supplies I'd taken from the store last night, I headed around the front of the house, leaving my car parked on the side. No sense in attracting attention after all. Elmer padded along behind me, growling his annoyance at the porch stairs but making it up them without help. The door swung open easily, and I led the way toward the pipe that needed a valve replacement.

Having grown up working in hardware stores, I knew a thing or two about home repairs. I didn't like to mess with gas or electricity too much because those things could cause fires or explosions. Not what I wanted. I was a pro at plumbing, though. Replacing a leaky valve was one of the easier projects I could do, especially since the invention of push-to-connect fittings. My acetylene torch could be used for spider-mice slaying instead of sweating copper pipes and fittings together. Bonus.

For about an hour, I worked in the back room, trying hard not to cause any more damage while still removing a segment of pipe and the corroded valve that could no longer hold water. Every now and again, I thought I heard footsteps above me. Groans and knocks from the second floor that broke my concentration and forced me to stop to listen harder. Settling. The house had to just be settling. The darn thing practically gave off a symphony of sounds whenever I walked through it, so additional noises didn't stand out as anything too terrifying. Plus, Elmer sat at my side as calm as ever. Since I sort of relied on the beast to be my early detection device, I assumed we were fine.

Still, the noises bothered me. Making the hair on the back

of my neck stand up and the air around me bubble with new emotion. Not so much sad as angry—hostile, even. Perhaps edging toward dangerous.

"You're paying attention, right?"

Elmer groaned, refusing to budge from his spot next to the bowl of water I'd gotten him. Poor guy was probably starving —neither one of us had eaten breakfast yet, and it was already quickly closing in on nine.

"Ten more minutes, buddy, then this should be done. If I did everything right, hopefully I can shower, and then we can mosey into town to grab some grub." As if either of us had ever moseyed in our lives.

It took about seven minutes to finish up and another two to run through the first floor and make sure the leaks all seemed to be stopped. No more water trickling down the walls, no puddles in the middle of the floor. Nothing but...well, humidity and water damage, but it could have been worse. Heck, when I didn't hear a single drip, I danced a jig across the foyer.

And that was the moment the sounds from upstairs definitely became footsteps. Even Elmer looked up at the noise and growled.

"Now you tell me."

I quickly evaluated my options—I was alone in the house with an unknown intruder, I had no real weapons, and no one would be looking for me for who-knew-how-long should I go missing. I, once again, made the only decision a woman in my position could.

I ran out the door and headed around the side of the house for my minivan.

As soon as I had Elmer in his seat and the engine started to make a fast getaway, I laid on the horn. Might as well scare whoever had invaded my space. Just as I expected, someone must have raced out of the house because I saw a flash of a person in the back—dark snapback on their head and wearing a nondescript tee—just before they disappeared behind the structure as they headed toward the woods. There had definitely been someone in the house with us. That didn't make me feel any better about taking ownership of the manor. Or staying there. Or...well, anything. Nothing was better.

"Okay. We're okay," I said, patting Elmer's head as my heart raced. I wasn't sure what to do—go inside and lock up? Leave and hope no one else invaded the place? Call the police?

Yeah, that last one seemed like the best idea. Except when I pulled out my phone and swiped the screen to life, I had no signal. Nothing. Nada. No Wi-Fi in the area either. Willow Manor was a dead zone. Wonderful.

The only option I saw as reasonable was to leave—drive into town, head for the hardware store, and call the local police from there. I didn't even feel comfortable enough to go lock the doors.

"I thought small towns were supposed to be safer, Elmer."

The dog didn't respond. Typical.

I put the van in drive and headed around the house, pointing the nose toward the road that would lead me back into downtown Reverie Springs. Leaving my new home completely open for all the world to access.

Looked like I was going to have to rely on people to not be thieving thieves, at least for a few hours. What was there to steal from such a dilapidated old home, anyway?

Chapter Four

I pulled up at the hardware store, but the building sat quiet and still, and Gwendolyn didn't answer when I rang the bell at the rear of the store. The old lady was probably out hexing townspeople. I could have tried to follow the scent of the potion she'd brewed the day before, but I really wasn't in the mood for chasing the woman around town. That decision didn't solve my problem, though.

Not wanting to be alone considering what we'd just gone through, I dragged Elmer with me to the diner instead of locking ourselves up in the store. Hopefully, I would find my aunt there having a late breakfast.

I, instead, found one very cranky chef.

"He can't come in here," the tall man said, pointing toward Elmer, who had already taken a seat outside next to the door.

"Yeah. I know. Have you seen Gwendolyn?"

That ever-present frown deepened, his beard moving with the change in expression. "Not today. Why?"

How to explain this one. "I realize this may sound strange, but I need to call the police about an intruder I saw out at my house, and I don't really want to be alone when I do that. Do you mind if I call from here?"

The man's entire demeanor shifted, the harsh edges surrounding him softening. It was a physical and emotional transformation I hadn't been expecting. One that set off a feeling inside me that I was not prepared for. His dark eyes met mine, holding strong and steady, and I felt as if the floor fell away. As if the world shifted just a bit, tilting entirely in his direction. I had to look away so I could stop the sensation.

What was *that*?

Apparently unaffected by whatever had sent my brain sideways, he guided me through the restaurant, calling over his shoulder as he directed me toward a table at the back. "Mary, bring a glass of water, please."

"On it, boss."

I took the seat the chef—Ander, if I remembered correctly from the day before—offered and smiled at Mary when she brought me the water. "Thanks. Do you know...should I call 9-1-1, or is there a nonemergency number?"

Ander grunted, recapturing my attention before he turned and strode toward the kitchen. "Give me a minute."

Mary twisted a towel that usually hung at her hip, looking nervous.

"I'm fine," I said as I reached for the water, smiling her way. "Really."

"I wouldn't be."

Before I could even come up with a response, Ander returned...with a basket of bread. That I had not ordered. I mean, I'd eat it, but...

"I just needed a number."

Ander pushed the bread closer to me. "I already called. The sheriff will be by in a few minutes. Eat something."

"Hang on. You called?"

He grunted, nodding once. "My restaurant, my rules."

Oh heck no. "My intruder, my phone call."

Mary grimaced, whispering, "Oh boy."

"You need help, and I'm helping you," Ander said with a shrug. "I would think you'd be grateful."

"That's not really how this works."

Ander wasn't budging, though. "It is with me."

Before I could fall deeper into my argument with the chef, the bell over the door rang, and I had to return to the reality of my own making. Living—and filing a police report—in Reverie Springs.

"Morning, Ander." The man in the brown uniform sidled over, looking about as unconcerned as any law enforcement official could and radiating an arrogance that chipped away at what kittle calm I had left. "You must be Miss Gwen's great-niece. Rylie, was it?"

I gripped the hand he offered, shaking once. "Brylie. But yes, I'm Gwendolyn's niece."

"Your aunt is a lovely woman. Been living here in Reverie Springs for going on seventy years now, if I remember right."

Probably closer to eighty, but no way was I going to out another woman's age. "Sure. So, about this morning—"

"Right. Ander said you claim someone was in your house." He pulled a pad of paper and a pen from his pocket before grabbing a pair of reading glasses from another and sliding them up his nose. "Where did you say you live again?"

"I didn't, but it was out at Willow Manor."

The sheriff's eyes darted to mine. The hard chill of suspicion, fear, and anger swirling around the man caught me by surprise. "You're living at Willow Manor?"

I dropped my gaze to avoid the sense of disbelief radiating from him, staring at the tabletop instead. "Yes."

"That's Miss Gwen's place."

So I'd heard. "She gave it to me."

He laughed, the sound grating. Even Ander turned to frown at the man.

"No one gives away a house," the sheriff said, still laughing. "Especially not one on as much land as the manor."

Ander slapped a mug of coffee down in front of the sheriff, stealing my attention. "I think what you want to know is who was in the house and why. Right, Sheriff?"

The sheriff coughed, looking decidedly uncomfortable all of a sudden, and reached for the mug. "Of course. Now, at what point this morning did you realize that there was someone in your house?"

And so it went—for forty-five minutes, I sat and answered what felt like two hundred questions about my morning. Where I'd been, what I'd been doing, why I hadn't investigated the noises from upstairs, what I'd seen and not seen. Mary thankfully checked on Elmer for me a few times, giving me a thumbs-up whenever she came back in so I knew he was okay. Ander cooked the entire time. I had no idea what, but it smelled delicious and made my stomach growl more than once. He also brought more coffee—for the sheriff and for me when I asked. I purposely kept my eyes on my cup when he came by, though. No way did I want to fall into the energy he exuded. Not with the sheriff sitting across from me and wanting to know way too much information.

"So, the person who ran—could you tell the gender?"

Question number #206, though it was probably the seventh time he'd asked it. "No. Again, I was too far away, and they moved fast enough for me not to get a good look. But they headed into the woods on the right side of the house."

"Is that the north or the south woods?"

I was seriously bad at directions, so that new question—#207—stumped me. "Uh..."

"North," Ander said, appearing like magic once more with his carafe of coffee. "If she was looking at the front of the house—as she has said she was—and the person ran to the right of the house, then they ran into the north woods. As you should know, Sheriff."

"Hmm." The sheriff frowned, looking over his notes, his irritation obvious. "Okay. Well, I guess I have enough for now. I'll head out there and look around. Make sure there's nothing too fishy going on."

And likely find nothing. Still, his trek out there didn't have to be a total waste of time.

"Could you..." I stopped, biting my bottom lip, unsure if this was something the police in town could even do. "I'm sorry to ask this, but could you maybe make sure the front door is locked? I didn't stop to do it, and I'd hate to leave the house wide open for more intruders."

"I will, of course, but I wouldn't worry about intruders. We haven't had a break-in in Reverie Springs in at least a decade."

A strong itch raced up my arm, the lie setting off every instinct I had for detecting bullshit. I fought the urge to claw at my forearm, frowning.

"Really?"

Ander grunted, obviously on the same wavelength. "Except last fall when the Morris boy was caught filching honey from old Ben's barn."

The sheriff laughed that annoying, arrogant laugh again. "That wasn't really a break-in."

All the way to my elbow—my goodness, did my arm itch. I couldn't help but scratch at it.

Ander shrugged, looking unaffected by the sheriff's dismissal. "He broke in to the barn to steal something, so I'd certainly call it a break-in."

"Well, we haven't had a home break-in, then." The sheriff shot me a smile, one that definitely didn't reach his eyes. One that fell when he caught me running my short nails over the reddened skin of my inner arm. "I'm sure you'll be fine."

Or I could be murdered in my sleep by whoever had been walking around upstairs in the manor. I had a feeling he wouldn't be bothered too much either way. Okay, maybe that was going too far. He'd be bothered by the paperwork, for sure.

"Thanks for your time," I said, rising to my feet and offering my hand to the sheriff to put an end to this interview. "I appreciate you going out to the manor to take a look around."

"It's no problem, Brylie. You tell your aunt I said hello, and that I was very purposefully *not* sending her any negativity this month."

Because of the hexes she brewed. I would have bet he'd been sprinkled with the potion of deathly stench many times over the years. And if the way my arm continued to itch was any indication, he wasn't telling the truth about not sending her negativity.

"I will. Thanks again."

I scratched my wrist and waited for him to leave before running to the door to check on Elmer, who lay sleeping in the shade with a bowl of water and...

"Who gave you a bone, buddy?"

"Ander told me to," Mary said as she stepped beside me. "He said your boy looked hungry. You do, too. Have you eaten anything other than bread yet?"

I shook my head, my eyes locked on that hunk of bone. Something about it, about the kindness of someone else stepping in to make sure Elmer was okay while I dealt with an uncomfortable reality, spoke to me. Maybe Gwendolyn had been right—maybe Ander was one of the nicer guys in town. Men could be grumpy and nice, right?

"Come on," Mary said, tugging me into the restaurant and leading me back to the table where I'd been sitting for so long. "What can I get you for breakfast? On me."

"Oh, no. I can pay for food."

She placed a hand on my shoulder, that warmth she exuded sinking all the way into my bones. "Let me help you. Now, what do you want to eat?"

I did not have the energy to attempt to fight her on such a silly thing, so I smiled instead. "I'll have the breakfast platter."

"Want your eggs scrambled?"

"Yes, please."

"You got it. Give Ander a few minutes to get that ready for you."

And with that, she disappeared into the kitchen, speaking quietly to Ander as he stood at the flat top. I took a sip of my water, needing a minute to catch my breath and settle my soul. One full day in Reverie Springs, and I'd already been dealt hexes, possible witchcraft, hybrid spider-mice, water damage, being scared by a nosy neighbor, and an intruder. I sort of wanted to know what would come next.

Which was a really stupid thought to have.

Have you ever heard the phrase, don't tempt fate? Yeah, even thinking about what would come next apparently did just that because the bell over the door rang, and the woman from the day before—the intoxicated, leash-law–loving lady—came storming inside.

"That dog is out there without a leash again." She hurried my way, an air of pure rage dancing around her. Rage and whiskey, if my nose was correct. "Did you not understand me last night?"

Oh, now see, I'd been raised to be a nice woman with good manners. I had a bit of a snarky sense of humor—*thanks, Dad* —but overall, I thought of myself as a kind person who tried really hard to control her temper. Unless you in any way implied that I was stupid. My tether tended to snap at the first indication that someone thought I wasn't capable of understanding them.

Like the woman standing before me apparently did.

"Are you seriously implying that I don't have the mental capacity to know what a leash law is?"

"Well, obviously, you don't because that animal is once again on the street without proper restraint." She stumbled a little, wobbling even closer as she pointed a long, manicured finger in my direction. "I should call animal control on you."

I was pretty sure Reverie Springs didn't even have an animal control department, not that it really mattered. "He's fine. He's not going to bother anyone."

"So you say." She huffed and shook her head as if she simply couldn't believe I would dare to do something as blatant as disregarding leash laws. Which I would—I was pretty sure Elmer had never been on a leash in his life.

I picked up a piece of bread, tearing off a chunk as I said, "Elmer won't bother anyone or go anywhere without me, so if we're done here, I'd like to eat my breakfast in peace."

That didn't seem to sit well with her. "I know who you are,

you know. You should be ashamed of yourself, stealing from the infirmed the way you have."

"Excuse me? Infirmed what?" Because infirm was an adjective, not a noun, and I no longer had any idea what the heck we were arguing about.

"Your aunt. Anyone who actually thinks they're some sort of witch and brews disgusting concoctions they call potions should be locked up, but that doesn't mean they should be stolen from."

Oh no, she didn't. She *did not* imply that one, my great-aunt was crazy—which she might well be, but that wasn't for some drunk lady with a leash grudge to decide—and two, that I was a thief. I'd never stolen a thing in my life—not even a piece of gum from the candy store. I wasn't about to accept that nonsense.

"Look, lady, I don't know who you think—"

Just then, the bell over the door rang again, stopping me in midsentence. Ander stood at the entrance, his thick frame taking up every inch of space, staring hard at the other woman while holding the door open...for Elmer.

"He's my guest," Ander said with a heavy frown on his face as my dog passed him to come sit under my table. "And I don't appreciate you coming in here and causing trouble because of Miss Gwen, Joan. You know how I feel about that."

Joan didn't seem ready to let anything go. "But that—"

"No," Ander said, shooting a quick glance my way that held more fire than I could have ever imagined. "You won't start this here."

Joan puffed up, looking ready to tear him a new one, but then she backed down as most bullies tended to do. "I'm telling you, whatever she's cooking up there should be illegal."

"Well, it's not, but harassing my patrons is." Ander glanced my way again, his eyes catching mine for one moment and sending a shot of something completely foreign barreling into my chest. What was that sensation, and how could he live with so much anger and heat inside him, so much intensity?

And why on earth was he turning that on Joan?

The woman shrank under his harsh gaze, sniffing and raising her chin as if she still held the power when we all knew that one glance had cut her off at the knees.

"Fine," she spat, trying hard to hang on to some bit of control. "I'll leave, but if I see that dog out again without a leash, I'm calling the sheriff."

"Go right ahead," I hollered, growing louder as she moved toward the door. "Or I'll do it for you—he was already here having coffee with me this morning."

Okay, so that sounded a little like I had more of a relationship with Mr. Starched-Uniform-Pants than I actually did, but that woman had gotten under my skin like no one else, and I had no interest in playing the nice girl.

Thankfully, Joan didn't reply, just shot me a glare over her shoulder and walked out the door, leaving me alone with Ander, Mary, and Elmer. The latter of whom promptly plopped against the table leg and began snoring. Darn dog.

But I still had more things than Elmer to worry about, including one cranky chef who'd done me a couple of really big favors.

"Thank you," I said, catching Ander's attention. "I appreciate you stepping in there."

"You're welcome." The gruff voice had disappeared, replaced with something softer and quieter. Less harsh. "You okay? I noticed you scratching at your arm."

I held out the offending limb, looking over the pink marks I'd left there. "Yeah. Just something that came up, but it seems to be gone now." I chuckled, smiling at him. "Maybe I'm allergic to the sheriff."

"Allergic to his BS is more my guess." Ander sighed, looking right at me. Enveloping me in a sense of quiet calm that I rarely experienced. At least until he pointed a spatula at Elmer and said, "If that dog gets even a single hair in my kitchen, I'm never letting you—or him—in here again."

That actually seemed pretty reasonable. "Understood. Though if you had a couple tables out there for alfresco dining, I wouldn't bring him in here at all."

"Well, I don't. So, sit inside." He turned as if to leave then spun back around, his face scrunched in an unreadable expression. "What do you feed him?"

"Dog food," I said with a shrug. "Bagged stuff."

Ander's grunt of disapproval practically echoed off the walls. "My sister says that stuff is all chemicals."

"And your sister knows this how?"

"She's a vet."

"Oh." Simple but perfect response. His sister really would know what she was talking about in that case. "Is she local?"

Because Elmer would need a vet eventually. Even if just for a checkup. But Ander shook his head.

"No." Hard answer in a hard voice, cutting off the conversation. "Mary will have your plate out here in a minute. I'll make the dog some eggs."

He turned as if to leave once more then stopped—again— and looked at the table where Elmer lay. Snoring, of course. Quite loudly, actually. "What's his name?"

"Elmer."

"Like Fudd?"

No, but that reference was always assumed and far easier to explain. "Sure."

Ander nodded. "Bacon, too. Dogs love bacon."

And with that, he finally headed back into the kitchen to make my dog breakfast, while I...well, I reclaimed my seat and took a couple really deep breaths before lifting my latest cup of coffee to my lips.

If I was going to have a day of craziness and absurdity, I might as well be extra caffeinated for it.

Chapter Five

It took me three days to dig through the paperwork at the hardware store. Thirty-six solid work hours of poring over notes and receipts and invoices. At the end of that, when I stood in the doorway to the office and looked at the clean desk surfaces and empty windowsills, I was completely and utterly infused with a feeling of accomplishment.

I mean, I still had no idea how Rose had run the business, but at least I didn't have to deal with the fear of being buried under a towering mountain of paper anymore. I'd consider that a win.

Plus, I had a true, functioning office. My tablet sat on one desk; a squishy bed for Elmer lay under the other. My dog, my business partner, and my protector. Sort of. I mean, he woke me up every morning when the temperature rose too high to stay in the van any longer, and I was pretty sure he'd at least growl if any sort of spirit or hexer came too close. That counted, right?

And yes, we were still sleeping in the van. The sheriff had stopped by the store the day I'd filed the report to let me know he'd taken a walk around the property and not seen anything unusual, that he'd locked up for me and left the house without a worry. His reassurances hadn't comforted me much. I still felt the deep heartache of the place, still shuddered under the weight of sadness there. I also couldn't forget the terror that had filled me when I'd realized the noises I'd been listening to had been from someone actually in the house with me. No thanks to reliving that feeling over and over again. My van was fine for sleeping, at least for the moment.

And my store still needed a ton of work. Work that made me miss my dad even more than usual since it was the sort of stuff he would have been excited about. Resets, remerchandising, trying new product layouts—he would have been in his glory helping me open my own store.

Instead, he was gone.

A thought that I pushed down and tried not to think about. "Come on, Elmer. Let's go check out the paint department."

The dog groaned as if I'd asked him to run a marathon, but he followed me through the aisles and to the department my dad had lovingly referred to as *the danger zone*. Chemicals of all sorts sat in metal containers along the shelves, with unopened cans of paint taking up the most space. Paint that hadn't been touched in five long years. This would likely be a complete gut job but one that had to be handled meticulously due to the nature of the products.

This was going to take some serious time and energy, both physical and mental. The last few years, my dad had run the front of the store, while I had handled all the back-end stuff. This—dealing with stocking the shelves and setting—made me think of him. Of our time spent together when the store had grown quiet or before we'd opened for the day. It made me remember him—made me miss him. I wasn't sure I was ready for that just yet, but it was time to try.

Before I could work up the mental fortitude to attack the chemical mess in front of me, a chime sounded, followed closely by a voice I was beginning to know quite well.

"Yoo-hoo, Brylie dear. Where are you?"

Only one woman I knew would say yoo-hoo in that high-pitched way. "I'm in the paint department."

I moved to the main aisle—the racetrack, as it should be called—with a grin unconsciously kicking up at the scene before me. Gwendolyn Laveau—of the Reverie Springs hexing Laveaus—practically pranced between the endcaps, smiling brightly. Her dark-gray outfit—was that a dress? A muumuu? An awful lot of fabric hung from her body, sheer gray layers that rose and fell with every step, giving off the impression of a weightless sort of floating train around her feet. Making it seem as if she had somehow figured out how to defy gravity and danced on air across the store with her long silver braid trailing behind her.

The woman was a sight. "Why are you dressed so pretty today, Aunt Gwendolyn?"

That moniker, the admission of a family bond, grated a little bit. Not because of Gwendolyn herself, but because I'd never called anyone aunt in my life. It would take a little time for me to get used to it. But the name brightened the woman's smile even more, as it always did, so I soldiered on.

Gwendolyn hurried toward me but didn't attempt to catch my eye, something I'd noticed her doing with intention. And something I definitely appreciated. "Oh, my sweet girl. Where have you been? I haven't seen you in an age."

Bright, bubbly, and completely full of crap. "We had dinner together two nights ago."

"Was that just two days ago?" She waved a hand in my direction. "I'm an old woman. I forget things. It felt like so much longer."

I had a feeling the woman never forgot a single thing, and the slight itchy sensation on my wrist confirmed that. "I bet. So what brings you down to the store today? Need some hardware?"

She laughed, a quiet sort of sound that forced my lips to turn up in response. "No, nothing needed. I just thought I'd come say hello."

"Right." The air practically vibrated with the energy of her lie, and the itch moved higher up my arm. No way did I believe that excuse. "Well, hello."

"Hello again, dear." She looked around the store, an air of sadness settling over her. Of missing pieces and loss. It made sense, of course—her friend had owned this place. Had run the store, with Gwendolyn helping or hanging around. I felt a similar sadness when I thought about my dad and how much I missed the little things about having his presence in my life. Two peas in a pod, Gwendolyn and I. Two people dealing with loss.

"I finished cleaning out the office," I said, scrabbling for some sort of small talk. "Rose's desks are—"

At the mention of her friend, Gwendolyn jerked my way. Looking right at me. Likely forgetting how much discomfort her gaze brought with it. The pain that lanced through me as she locked her light eyes on mine stole my breath.

"Gwendolyn." I choked, bringing my hand to my throat and stumbling backward a step.

Thankfully, the old lady seemed to understand what was happening. She looked to the floor, releasing me from her emotions. "I'm sorry. I sometimes forget how strong that is for you."

It rubbed me the wrong way that she could forget something I couldn't even understand. "What *is* that? Why do I...feel it?"

"It's your gift, my dear."

The words my father had made me say a million times came exploding from my mouth. "I don't have a gift."

Gwendolyn's eyebrows winged up, the question clear. The implication obvious.

I ignored those gray arches of truth. "Why does looking at you specifically hurt so much?"

"Ah." She tugged at the airy fabric around her hips, her lips twisting into something close to a frown. "That's a long story, and one meant for another day."

"But—"

"Why don't you come upstairs with me?" She pasted a smile on her face, one that didn't match the remaining sense of sadness around her. One that I didn't believe was true. "We can have lunch together."

I checked out the number of chemicals needing to be sorted behind me, fighting the urge to run away from the mess, even if just for an hour or so. *Must be an adult.* "I have a lot of work to do, so I shouldn't."

"Work will be there when you're done. Besides, I have a big pot of stew on the stove and some crusty bread from Ander's diner. Much of that will go to waste if I don't have company."

I mean...wasted food was practically a crime. Starving children and all that. Plus, the thought of a big pot of homemade stew and fresh bread had me fighting back the drool. Still, my dad had raised me to never ask for things I hadn't earned.

"I hate to be a bother."

"You will never be a bother, child." Gwendolyn leaned closer, lowering her voice as if conspiring with me. "I even have good, homemade butter for the bread. Let me feed you and Elmer."

Elmer stood up and padded over, looking up to the old woman as if he'd understood every word she'd said and had fallen in love with her because of her generosity. And maybe he had—Aunt Gwendolyn seemed to like to feed my dog. As did Ander, who'd made Elmer a plate at breakfast yesterday when I'd stopped in for a quick cup of coffee that had turned into a three-course meal. Elmer was never going to eat kibble again, it seemed.

He also wasn't going to forgive me if I refused him beef stew. "Well then, sure. Lunch sounds really great."

"Excellent. I'm so thrilled to have you," she said, looking and sounding as if she meant it. No harm in making an old lady happy, I guessed.

Gwendolyn led the way through the store and into the storage area, unlocking another door that opened into a brick-walled hallway with wooden stairs painted in bright colors. We climbed to the second floor, that gray frock she wore bouncing and floating before me over the lime-green, chartreuse, and lemon-yellow treads. I couldn't tear my eyes away even as we transitioned to orange and hot pink, to deeper reds and purples. Seriously, how did that fabric *do* that? Just...hang in mid-air? I couldn't stop staring at it. Couldn't stop noticing how it lifted on its own and simply never dropped back down.

Which was how I almost—*almost*—ran right into the giant cow's head mounted on the wall at the top of the stairs.

"Holy crap." I froze, too afraid of falling to back up. Too terrified of being gored by the horns on that thing's head to move in any direction. Forward was definitely out—the head was practically nose-to-nose with me. Snout? Nose-to-snout sounded better in my head.

Aunt Gwen apparently took my exclamation as more positive than I'd intended. "Isn't he beautiful?"

Nope. Not the word I'd been thinking at all. "He's...something."

"That's Cletus. He used to live in a pasture near Willow Manor and would follow Rosie around when she was gardening. She would complain about that bull every single day." Gwen laughed and patted the side of the head of the beastly bull. Not cow. I should have known that by the horns. Not that I had much experience with bovine.

"Why is he here?"

Gwendolyn opened the door to the apartment, giving Cletus a slight smile before grabbing my elbow and leading me inside with a tug. Intersection with the bull avoided. "Rose complained and complained about that bull, but when he stopped showing up, she worried. And when she found out he was sick and likely dying, she walked over to that farmer and bought him on the spot. Cletus made it another four months under Rose's care, and when he passed, she threw him a full Irish wake—whiskey and all."

Reverie Springs got weirder and weirder with every story. "So, what...he died, so she had him stuffed?"

"No, dear. The town did."

Aaaannnddd...weirder. "The town. Like, people paid for that?"

"They certainly did. Paid for it, helped Ander find a taxidermist who would mount him, and donated the head to Rose so she never had to be without her friend."

I blinked, the words not really making sense. And yet, there was something in them—something unsaid. Something I sensed from more than just the story of Cletus the bull.

"It sounds like the residents of Reverie Springs really cared for Rose."

"Oh, they did, dear. They truly did. She was an angel among us." Gwendolyn sniffed, closing her eyes for just a moment before pasting that fake smile back on and waving me into the kitchen. "Come now. Let's have some beef stew."

Beef. As in bovine. As in... "It's not Cletus stew, is it?"

The laugh that escaped the old woman filled the entire room and practically sparkled in the air. "Of course not. No one ate Cletus. Rose wouldn't hear of it."

Of course not, because he had been like a pet to her. Speaking of which, Elmer had followed me up the stairs and into the apartment only to quite literally fall under a table. And snore.

"Your dog is something else," Gwendolyn said as she ladled steaming stew into two bowls.

"He is, but I love him."

"As well you should. Just be careful with him around town —dogs aren't as well received here as in other places." She sat at the table, indicating I should take the chair across from her. Fresh bread—crusty and golden brown—sat on a board between us with a pot of soft butter beside it. The stew was dark and thick, with big chunks of meat and vegetables apparent. And the smell—much better than hexing day.

"So, what do you want to know?" Gwendolyn asked, spoon in her hand, giving me a knowing look.

I tugged a piece of bread from the slice she'd provided me. "About what?"

"Anything—the store, the manor, your mother. You have my undivided attention. Ask me anything."

"Will you tell me the truth if I do?"

"Truth is relative," she replied with a shrug. "I'll tell you what I can, though."

I gave her offer some serious thought. There was a lot that I wanted to know about her and Rose, about the manor, about my mother. So much to learn. And yet I had a sense that there was a time frame in which some of that information needed to come to me. A feeling that I wasn't ready for the heaviest parts yet. So I picked what I considered the safest topic.

"The townspeople call you Miss Gwen. Do you prefer that over Gwendolyn?"

"Heavens, no. It's a nickname the teachers gave me back when I was in high school and they didn't feel like using my entire name. You'll find out soon enough—things stick around here."

"Then I'll call you Aunt Gwendolyn."

She grinned. "Thank you. I appreciate that."

Next topic. "Who are all the pictures of in the manor? The ones lining the hallways on the main floor."

Gwendolyn practically lit up. "Those are all Rose's ancestors. She loved genealogy and tracked her family tree endlessly. There's one in the powder room of her great-great-great-grandfather, who originally bought the manor. It's my favorite."

I frowned, knowing exactly what room she meant. "There is no portrait in the powder room."

"Of course there is. I hung that picture myself."

I shrugged, already halfway finished with my stew and somehow not remembering that I'd taken a single bite. "Well, perhaps it got lost along the way with the hardware and doors."

Gwendolyn set her spoon down, her frown deepening. "What are you talking about? What doors?"

"The ones that are missing."

"Nothing should be missing from that house. It was pristine when I closed it up."

Five years before. A long time for people to notice the manor had been abandoned. "There're a lot of things that seem to be missing. Plus, with all the water damage—"

"What water damage?"

I finished the last bite of my stew, my stomach clenching uncomfortably at the anger in Gwendolyn's tone. "Well, you see, when I walked into the place, there was a water leak."

She made a sound like a hiss, sitting back. Her face hard with masked fury. "That is not possible."

Tell that to my warped wood floors. "Oh, it's possible. That leak was also a bear and a half to find. I'm still not sure I've gotten everything repaired because I come home to water on the floor quite often. And then when the person broke in the other day—"

"Broke in? To the manor?"

"Yeah. You didn't know?"

Because I hadn't told her. I hadn't said much about it since the sheriff had told me it was okay to be inside the house again. I'd been so busy and felt so stupid for not feeling safe there.

Apparently, Gwendolyn didn't appreciate my keeping secrets. "I want to know what's missing," she said, rising to her feet and carrying her bowl to the sink. "Every single piece of hardware or picture. Tell me everything."

"I can try, but considering I'm not sure what was supposed to be there and what wasn't, that might be tricky."

Gwendolyn grew silent and still, staring out the window. She seemed lost in thought, stuck in a place that brought her age to the forefront. That forced her wrinkles to deepen and the wear and tear of a woman who'd lived through too much to show.

She finally sighed, sounding older than I'd ever heard her as she said, "Take me there."

I nearly dropped the bread I'd been nibbling on. "Excuse me?"

Gwendolyn tossed her napkin on the counter and faced me with the bravest, most warrior-like expression on her face. Old woman replaced by fiery goddess ready to go to war. "Take me there. I'll help you determine what's missing. I can't imagine why anyone would steal from my dear Rose, but if they did, I need to know who."

The sense of determination, of anger, washed through me. This was Gwendolyn without the wall of sadness blanketing her, and she was a beautiful sight.

"Let me wake up Elmer, and we'll go."

Chapter Six

The house sat still and unassuming in the dappled afternoon sunlight, overgrown vines hanging from the eaves, sweet purple flowers peeking through the grass and weeds in the beds under the front windows, the porch shaded and inviting. Slightly messy, but totally devoid of any sense of malice. Still, I knew all that negativity bubbled under the surface. As with a rip current, the top layer appeared calm and perfect for swimming, but the danger lurked beneath.

I had no interest in being pulled out to sea.

"Are you sure you want to go in there?"

Gwendolyn made a sound like a huff, already reaching for the handle to her door. "It's just a house, Brylie."

Yeah. Right. Just a house that seemed to hate me and made my stomach hurt every time I walked inside.

"Okay, then." I scratched at the itch tickling my wrist—seriously, I was going to need to find a dermatologist soon—and stepped out of the van, opening the sliding door so Elmer could follow along with us. No way was I leaving him behind, no matter how big of a sigh he issued at being forced to move his chubby body. Apparently, I'd interrupted his second (third?) afternoon nap. The poor dog.

"Tell me more about the break-in," Gwendolyn said as she looked over the front of Willow Manor. "I want to know everything."

"Not much to tell. I was inside working on the plumbing issues and kept hearing weird noises. I assumed it was the house settling—"

"It is an old house."

"But then there were definite footsteps. Even Elmer growled."

She glanced at the dog, who had sat at my feet with a bored expression on his face. "Maybe he was just snoring."

As if I didn't know the difference. "Nope, definitely a growl. I ran outside and hopped into the van so I could honk the horn."

"Why would you honk the horn?"

"To scare the person inside."

"Why would you want to scare them?"

"Uh...to make them leave?"

She blinked, looking decidedly confused by my actions, which did sound a little odd in retrospect. "Okay, so footsteps."

"Right, and when I honked the horn, someone went running out the back door and into the woods."

"Which woods?"

I pointed. "Those ones."

She frowned. "Thomas Lee lives over that way, but I can't see him breaking in to this house. He's been renting the fields of the manor for years."

"I couldn't tell you anything about the person who ran, and when the sheriff came out—"

"The sheriff was here?"

"Yeah. I drove back to town and called the police from the diner."

"Why didn't you come to my apartment?"

"You weren't home."

She looked pensive for just a moment before nodding in an exaggerated way. "Right—it's been a very busy hexing week for me."

Of course it had. "Well, that's why I called from the diner. The sheriff came and took my statement. He also drove out here to look around and lock up for me since I wasn't comfortable coming back."

"It's your home. You should feel comfortable here."

"Yeah, well—uninvited strangers coming into the house while I'm here alone makes for uncomfortable moments."

"Stran-*gers*?"

I frowned. "Yes, strangers. Why?"

"Because that's plural, but you only saw one thief."

Right. "They weren't the first, though. I met another neighbor the other night after he stood on the porch and stared inside for a while."

"Which neighbor?"

"Carl."

She huffed and waved her hand. "He's a harmless old coot."

"I'm sure he is—" *I was also sure he'd hate to hear someone describe him that way* "—but he still walked in here uninvited after watching me through a window. It wasn't fun."

She patted my hand, something close to a feeling of laughter surrounding her. "Of course it wasn't."

Oh, heck no. She was not about to placate me. "He scared me."

"I'm sure he did, dear. Why, I'd likely be scared to death by an elderly man at my window as well."

My arm burned, the need to scratch it only making my temper shorter. I really did hate it when people lied to me. "You act like it's normal for people to come and go as they please in this house. Is it a private residence or a public building?"

"It's a private residence—yours, to be precise."

"Then I am the one to decide who comes in and who doesn't. You don't get to mock me because you know and trust all these people—I don't. I was alone in a strange area with no phone service, and he strolled right in as if he owned the place. He scared me."

Gwendolyn's face fell, her expression changing to one of regret. "Understood, my dear. I forget how long I've been here sometimes and how well I know all of these people. I know Carl would never hurt you, but you don't, and I can see how his sudden presence inside your home would be disturbing. I'm sorry for brushing that off. It won't happen again."

I doubted that, but at least she'd apologized. "Fine. So... what do you want to do now?"

She looked over the exterior—the dark, heavy carriage lights darkened with dirt and grime, the front door whose paint had chipped and faded, the filthy windows. All of it needing some tender loving care. All of it likely reminding her of happier times.

I wanted to bring the house back to rights, even if it was just to wipe the sad look off this woman's face.

She finally sighed, nodding toward the door. "Let's go inside and see if we can figure this thing out so you can feel more comfortable here. I want you to get to know the manor a little better."

Go inside. Into the house of pain and sadness. Sure thing—I'd get right on that. I really wanted to pull an Elmer and sigh in exhaustion and frustration when we started moving toward the house, but I wasn't a dog. I was a human. I kept that stuff inside and did what was expected of me.

Gwendolyn led the way onto the porch, the coolness of the shaded space a welcome respite from the midday sun that had been beating down on us. What I wouldn't give to throw open every window of the house and let the breeze dance through the rooms as I cleaned, but I couldn't. Not with missing screens and people breaking in. I couldn't even sleep in the house; how was I supposed to trust leaving it vulnerable to the outside world that way?

"Are you sure about this?" I asked, voicing the question that had to be asked. Not sure if I was more worried about her mental state or my own.

"Open it, Brylie."

I stared at Aunt Gwendolyn, wanting to understand the hesitancy in her voice, the sense of fear I picked up from her. The sadness was back too. So heavy, and such a burden to live under. There was nothing I could possibly say to ease the pain I knew she was dealing with, so instead, I did as I was told. I unlocked the front door and swung it open, allowing Gwendolyn to walk inside first.

The wave of total and utter desolation that hit me upon stepping inside nearly knocked me to my knees. I didn't even have to look into Gwendolyn's eyes to feel it, didn't have to glance her way to pick up on the emotions pouring over her. Even Elmer whimpered under the deluge of Aunt Gwendolyn's energy as she walked into Willow Manor. Gwendolyn, though, simply kept moving, putting one foot in front of the other, with her chin up and her hands clasped in front of her. A picture of strength in the face of almost unbearable agony.

What was it about this place that caused such devastation to her mood?

"The floors look horrible." Gwendolyn's voice came out soft and rough, a little off from the norm. Not weak, though. No. Not that. "And the wallpaper. Rose spent months searching for just the right one for this foyer. She'd be heartbroken to see the place in such disarray."

"The floors are warped because of the water. I'll likely have to replace most of the wood. The wallpaper—" *wasn't really my style but fit the era of the house and seemed like something that was important to her* "—might be salvageable with some good adhesives."

She nodded, visibly swallowing. "Yes. That seems possible. I can help you fix it if you'd like. I helped Rose install it all."

I'd been right—she had a personal connection to the paper. I'd definitely be researching how to fix the delamination happening and get the pattern to line back up.

Aunt Gwendolyn walked deeper into the house, touching a light switch here and running her fingers along the odd frame there as the floors squeaked and moaned beneath her feet. Every picture almost seemed to hang a little straighter as she moved past them, and the lengthy hallway appeared to be growing lighter instead of darker with every passing moment. And when Gwendolyn entered the kitchen, when she stepped into the large room at the very back of the house with the greenhouse-like conservatory off to the side, a groan filled the space. A noise of settling, most likely, even if it did sound as if the house were sighing in some sort of relief.

"The handles..." She shook her head, practically petting the stone countertops and reaching for the naked cabinet fronts. "They were such lovely handles."

I wouldn't know because they were gone, likely stolen. A fact that made my heart hurt for the manor and for Great-Aunt Gwendolyn. "I'm sure they were."

She sighed, her steps growing faster. Her moves more determined. "That back pantry should have a door. There had been an antique print of different medicinal herbs on it. Rose had found it on our last birthday trip together and I hung it on the door so she would see it daily."

The house groaned again, a deeper sort of sound than before. More painful, almost. My gut clenched as a wave of sadness and anger collided inside me—not from me, though. I'd have been more prepared to deal with the feelings had they been my own.

I took a deep breath, nearly swaying under the emotions swirling in the room. "Maybe we can find another copy of it. I can go online to search if you can describe it to me."

She nodded once. "I can describe it. We'll need to locate a door first. Maybe Gleaves can help—he's good with his wood."

Which was a statement I would address another day. "You know a man named Gleaves?"

"Of course. Gleaves Philander. He lives on the next farm down from Carl and has a woodworking shop. He made some of the trim pieces for Rose when she was restoring this place."

His name was Gleaves, and he was good with his wood. Reverie Springs could not get any weirder.

And still, I was stuck on the person who'd been in the house with me. "You think Gleaves could be the thief?"

"Oh, no. He's not that kind of man. He reads poetry."

I closed my eyes, trying hard to rein in the sarcastic

response that had begun to fight its way out of my mouth. "So, if not Gleaves, the poetry-reading woodworker, who?"

"I have no idea. No one in town would steal from me."

"Are you sure about that?"

She froze, her eyes meeting mine. Filled with shock and surprise and...hurt. Not the pain I usually felt from her—this was newer. Less crushing and more stinging in a way. This was progress.

Aunt Gwendolyn lifted her chin. "Some people don't appreciate those who are different from what they consider normal."

Which was a nice way of saying there were people in town who likely didn't approve of her witchy, hex-brewing ways. People like Joan, the dog-leash inspector.

"Let's write down some names. People for me to look into."

Aunt Gwendolyn paused for just a moment before nodding. "I'll get a pen."

Two hours, a few sheets of paper, and a lot of stories about the residents of Reverie Springs later, I had a list of four people who may or may not have been the ones to break in to Willow Manor and steal the fixtures and antiques. A list Aunt Gwendolyn continued to fret over.

"I just don't know," she said as she followed me up the stairs to the second floor of the house. "I'm not sure Mike would be the type of person to disrespect me like that."

The Mike she spoke of was Mike Allen, a younger man

who had been the weekly delivery driver for the wholesaler Rose had bought from, someone who had always seemed interested in the goings-on of the manor rehabilitation, and the recent purchaser of a house far outside what Aunt Gwendolyn thought he should be able to afford. In other words, suspect number one.

"I'm not saying he is, but if it's possible he could be, we should keep our eyes on him." I walked from room to room, looking for a way to the mysterious third floor while also cautiously checking for leaks and puddles. So far, so waterless—other than the foyer, of course. Stupid powder room leaks.

But the second floor remained dry...and quiet. The floors suddenly seemed to creak a lot less, and the lights glowed just a little bit brighter. The malaise I'd experienced at the house for days was no longer present and instead had been transformed into something warmer and brighter. Something that felt more comforting.

If I had been okay with anthropomorphizing the structure, I would have said the house seemed happy.

Great-Aunt Gwendolyn was not. "But he's such a nice young man, and maybe he really had been interested in historic homes."

Or maybe he had been interested in expensive, historic architectural elements he could sell for a quick buck. "If it's not him, he'll never even need to know we were investigating him. But honestly, someone took the mantel from the fireplace. You said yourself that the thing weighed a ton and was an unwieldy hunk of wood. I can't see a lot of people being able to handle removing that on their own."

She sighed. "He is very strong and muscular."

As she'd said. More than once. "See? It's totally reasonable for us to look a little deeper into what he's been up to lately. Or we can hand over a list of the missing items to the sheriff and let him handle things."

"That ignorant pile of dung? The man has been nothing but useless since he was a child. You know he got held back in kindergarten for his lack of social skills? No thank you."

And so, our own investigation was off to a great start. Four people, all locals, who Aunt Gwendolyn thought were filled with enough negativity or who had shown an unusually strong interest in Willow Manor over the years. The list included Mike the delivery driver, the farmer who rented the fields, a real estate agent, and—oddly enough—Rose's sister. Joan. Of the dog-leash police variety.

I had not been surprised at that one.

"Okay," I said, standing in the empty hall with my hands on my hips. "This is it, right? We've covered every inch of the second floor."

"Yes, Brylie. Every inch."

"So then, where are the stairs to the third floor?"

Aunt Gwendolyn's face grew paler. "Why would you need to go up to the third floor?"

Why, indeed. "Because I own the house and want to know what's up there."

"It's basically an attic that Rose converted into a bedroom suite, but the one on the second floor is much nicer."

"I want to see the one on the third floor."

She sighed, her energy waning. Growing more cautious and wary. "The stairs are behind that door."

I followed her raised arm, opening the skinny door next to the entrance to the main bathroom that I had assumed to be a linen closet. Or, at least, trying to.

"It's locked."

"There is no lock on that door."

"Then it's stuck because I can't open it."

"Or maybe it doesn't want to be opened." Aunt Gwendolyn grabbed my arm, stopping me. "Today is not the day to face that room. Come. Let's head back downstairs. It's late, and I'd like to go home."

I didn't follow her down the stairs, though. Didn't stop trying to open the door that wasn't locked yet wouldn't open. I couldn't. The lack of movement made no sense. The door didn't look swollen and there were no obvious signs of why the slab seemed trapped in the frame, and yet, it simply wouldn't open.

As much as it should have worked, it didn't.

And if that wasn't a metaphor for what life was like for me in Reverie Springs, I didn't know what was.

Chapter Seven

My first week in Reverie Springs passed in a quiet sort of way, sans the whole someone-broke-in-to-my-house thing. I'd worked on the house that still leaked for no reason, toiled in the store, and learned a little bit about the downtown area. Like that there wasn't much *to* the downtown area.

There also wasn't a whole lot of traffic—foot or vehicle variety—headed down Main Street on a weekday afternoon. To be honest, there wasn't much on the weekends either, but the workweek seemed decidedly slower. I walked along the treelined street with Elmer by my side—sans leash, as always—trying hard to get both a little exercise and loosen our stiff muscles. Sleeping in my car had been doing a number on my back, a fact that I was going to have to deal with...and soon. Unloading the paint department of all the chemical containers and slinging old paint cans wasn't helping the situation.

I should have started in plumbing. I could chuck some PVC pipe fittings with ease.

"Pardon me." A blond man with a fake smile and the

whitest teeth I'd ever seen stopped me from the bench where he sat, leaning closer than was customary, in my opinion. "You do know there are leash laws in this town, right?"

In timing I couldn't have asked for, a squirrel jumped from one of the maple trees in front of us, walked right up to Elmer as if on a suicide mission, and then skittered away. Unharmed. Unchased, too. Elmer was far too busy lying on the concrete as if our slow walk in the shade had killed him.

Lazy beast.

"Yeah, I'm not so certain he needs one."

"Every dog needs one." Smiley frowned at my snoring dog. "What breed is he?"

"Basset hound."

The man nodded, his perfectly coiffed hair rising and falling with the motion as if hair-sprayed into place and not quite holding. I couldn't look away from it.

"Hounds are scent animals. He could run off on you if he decides to follow a trail."

"The only thing he'd follow is a bacon truck, and since there's no such thing, I'm sure we're fine."

"Suit yourself." He sat back, looking me up and down. Likely taking in my worn-out tennis shoes, ripped jean shorts, and faded tank and making up opinions about me. He seemed the type. "You're new in town. Reverie Springs has a small but very upscale rental market. How'd you find a rental you could afford without help?"

I raised an eyebrow at him and his expensive shoes. Fine. So I wasn't exactly dressed to impress, but that didn't mean he could judge me on my work wardrobe. This guy and his classist microaggressions, along with his cut-rate Karamo Brown-inspired bomber jacket, could go smell one of Elmer's farts.

"I don't rent—I own."

His head jerked up, that hair flying high in the breeze and his eyes locking on mine. Ooh, he was a slimy one all right—determined, too—and he had his sights set on something to do with me. Great.

"I've never seen you around, so you definitely haven't been here long. What agent did you use?"

"Agent of what?"

"Real estate...who sold you your house? Was it that Shelly chick with Red Roof Realty? Because she doesn't show the quality listings in the area. Did you buy some foreclosure or tax sale lot?"

"No." I left it at that as I took a step back, needing to escape. Ready to leave the guy behind and head back to the safety of the closed hardware store. Unfortunately, the man seemed to be a bit tenacious.

"Not a foreclosure? Then what, because I know every listing in this town and nothing has sold in weeks."

I had a feeling if I kept walking away, he'd follow me, so I stopped and crossed my arms over my chest. "I moved in to a house my great-aunt owned. She gifted it to me."

That seemed to catch his attention. He stepped closer again, looking decidedly more interested in me all of a sudden. "Are you Gwen Laveau's niece? The one who's moved in to Willow Manor?"

Something in his tone made me want to lie—not that I would. "Yes."

He reached out his right hand, suddenly much more smiley. "Lamb. Corbin Lamb."

Like Bond. James Bond. But also, one of the names on our list of possible suspects. Things had just taken a turn for the interesting. "I'm Brylie Scott."

That smile grew a little wider. "I've been meaning to come

say hello. As Reverie Springs's most successful real estate agent, I figured you and I should really become friends."

"And why is that?"

He turned that smile up another megawatt. "For when you sell the manor, of course."

Oh no. I had a feeling I was in danger of receiving...a sales pitch. From a man who, just two minutes ago, thought I couldn't afford to pay rent in this town. The horror. Good thing I knew how to stop this conversation in its tracks.

"I'm not selling the manor."

Too bad Corbin didn't know how to take no for an answer.

"Not yet, no, but someday." He made a move to wrap his arm around my shoulder, but a sharp dodge from me—and a strong growl from Elmer, who had definitely woken up and started paying attention—cut him off. He dropped his arm, his smile faltering a bit. "That house is way too much for a single woman. The upkeep, the cost of the utilities, all the cleaning— it's a nightmare. I tried to tell Gwen the same thing after Rose died, but she wouldn't listen. I certainly hope you're a smarter woman than your aunt."

This guy was a real piece of work. That shot Corbin had just fired? A direct hit on my family.

I edged farther away from him, seething inside. "Aunt Gwendolyn loves that house."

"She does, she does. But emotions and money are bad bedfellows. Rose and Gwen wouldn't listen to me about that."

Why he brought Rose into our conversation, I had no idea. But I didn't like it.

"Gosh, I wonder why." *Sarcasm, thy name is Brylie.*

"Exactly." He laughed, braying like a donkey and being way too loud. If anyone had actually been outside, they probably would have turned and looked. "So you see where I'm coming from. You're a smart girl, and I am here to tell you that I can get you a pretty hefty sum for the manor. We can divide up the land, sell off parts and pieces for new development, then put the house itself on the market and bring in some of those historic home buyers with deep pockets. You'll make a fortune."

"And you'd make one heck of a commission."

"Right," he said, still smiling. Still not picking up the irritation I would have thought was obvious. "It's a win-win situation. Everyone gets what they want."

Except Aunt Gwendolyn, who likely only wanted her friend back. I understood that feeling; I would have given anything for just one more day with my dad. And while I couldn't give her that—couldn't bless her with time—I could help preserve the memories she held dear.

And I would. Starting now. "Yeah, sorry, but I'm not selling the manor. Ever."

"Rylie, listen. I'm sure—"

"It's Brylie."

He froze, that smile going plastic and even more fake. "What?"

"My name. It's Brylie. You called me Rylie."

"No, I didn't."

"Yes, you did."

"No. I'm certain you misheard me," he said, shaking his head. And then he laughed.

My temper, it was not amused.

Gaslighting 101: never let them believe they heard or saw what they know they did.

"Look, Colton—"

"It's Corbin."

"No, it's not." I raised a finger to quiet him when he

opened his mouth. "Willow Manor is not for sale now, nor will it be in the near future. And even if I did decide to sell, I wouldn't be coming to a man who refuses to apologize for getting my name wrong. Now, if you'll excuse me, I have a date with a salad that shouldn't taste as good as it does. The lettuce here is delicious, and Ander puts these crunchy sweet things with it that I can't get enough of. The man is a food genius—who knew?"

And with that, I spun on my heel and strode toward Ander's diner, whistling for a very tired and irritated Elmer to follow me. Thankfully, he did...all the way to the diner and in through the front door. Ander may not have invited my dog in specifically since the day with the sheriff, but he also never complained that my hound ended up under my table whenever I ate there.

If he didn't want my dog inside the restaurant, he'd say something, right? Right.

"Hi, Mary," I said as I took my usual table in the back. "How's it going?"

"Good, Brylie. Everything here is good." She hurried over, already smiling and bringing that warm, friendly energy with her. "How's the manor? You getting all settled in?"

I wanted to say yes, but my back screamed no. "It's a slow process, but I'm sure I'll be moved in in no time."

Just as soon as I figured out who had been breaking in to the house and why.

"Well, good. That's real good. Now, is it a burger or a salad day?"

Such a simple question but one that I was excited to answer. "Salad. I've been craving those little coated nut things Ander puts in his salad with the strawberries."

Mary leaned closer, dropping her voice as if telling me a

secret from the grand total of two other patrons. "Some nights, he makes too many, and I get to take home the extras. I eat them like a dessert."

Scandalous. "No."

"Yes." She grinned. "They're so yummy."

They were, but her giddiness at such a simple thing was even more delicious.

"You are a lucky woman."

"Don't I know it." With a wink, Mary walked back toward the kitchen, hollering my order to a very busy—and surly-looking—Ander.

As I waited for my ridiculously tasty salad, I pulled out my phone and looked over my list of thievery suspects. Corbin Lamb was on there, and now that I'd met him, I could see why. What a moose knuckle. But at the same time, he seemed smarmy and not very into the physical sort of work that would be required to remove something like the fireplace mantel. I wasn't knocking him off the list, but I had my doubts as to his participation.

"Your salad." Ander—not Mary—placed the huge bowl of delicious greens, berries, cheese, and nuts before me, looking just as unhappy as ever.

Me? I was suddenly happier than I'd been in a week. "You added extra nuts."

"No, I didn't."

I raised an eyebrow, looking up at him and refusing to retreat from what I knew was true even when his cranky attitude rained down on me. "I have had this salad six times now, and this is definitely more nuts than usual."

He shrugged, looking decidedly uncomfortable. "Maybe I *was* a little heavy-handed with them."

Such a grumpster.

"You were, for sure." I grinned, unable not to notice how awkward he seemed about the whole thing. "Thank you—they're my favorite part."

He leaned closer, suddenly looking almost shy. "Sometimes I make an extra-large batch so Mary can take a bag home with her. She likes them as much as you do."

Oh, he had a heart, and his love language was acts of service...specifically around food. A fact he'd shown a few times, even if he was still more cranky than not. I liked knowing such things about him, though.

"That's very nice of you, Ander. You're a sweet man."

He grunted, standing up once more and taking a step away. "Yeah, well, I don't know about all that. How's Elmer doing?"

Subject change—accepted. I dipped to the side, craning my neck to peek under the table at the ball of fur snoring at my feet. "He seems to be doing just fine. Though he did get a little scolding from your local real estate agent."

Ander's brow tightened. "You met Corbin Lamb?"

"I did, and he didn't appreciate Elmer being all leashless and dangerous."

He laughed, the sound booming. "That dog is no more dangerous than Mary over there."

Again, he wasn't wrong. "Yeah, well, Corbin didn't seem to be a good judge of character. Or much else."

Like if a person could afford rent. That one still stung.

Ander stepped a little closer, lowering his voice as if telling me a secret. "Corbin Lamb is an ignorant blowhard. Don't take anything he says to heart."

I nodded, pushing aside the residual sting of dealing with Corbin and refocusing on the people I was starting to really appreciate. Like Ander and Mary...especially Ander.

"Thanks. I'm okay. The guy just irked me. I won't let him get under my skin again."

"Good. That's good." Ander grabbed the towel hung over his shoulder and swung it to the other one as he rocked his weight from one foot to the other. He looked ready to say something more when the phone—the one literally attached to the wall—began to ring. The shrill jangling made Ander's frown return with a vengeance. "I need to get that and do some work. Enjoy your salad."

He left without another word, not looking back. Not stopping until he had reentered his kitchen, reclaimed his domain of fire and spice, and picked up that darn landline.

Me? I dove into the salad that should not have tasted as good as it did. I swear, the man put something magical and addictive in it.

Something that kept me coming back for more every day.

Something that made me like the grumpiness of the local diner chef.

Who knew my name was Brylie, not Rylie.

And who was definitely not on the list of possible thieves.

Chapter Eight

A hardware store could be a lot of things—a place for the community to come together, a beacon of hope in the dark times of a home repair project, a center for knowledge and information. It could also be a complete mess of products that would never be purchased and boxes so covered in dust, they might as well have started rolling along the tile floor. Mine was unfortunately the latter.

"Quit fighting me, Elmer. This is for your own good. There is stuff here that could kill you."

The dog rocked his head again, trying hard to make me stop attacking him with the dust mask I'd cut and adjusted to fit his long snout. Thankfully, I had about a hundred pounds on him, so I won the battle. Basset hound lungs—protected.

"It's time to clear out the soil addendum aisle," I said as I secured my own mask in place. "Between the dust and the chemicals, this isn't a time to be particular about fashion. It's time to be smart."

He did *not* look as if he cared. Though, did he ever?

We headed out of the office and across the back room,

pushing through the swinging doors onto the sales floor without pause. But the second I turned the corner and looked up the main aisle of the store, I definitely paused. Even my heart followed suit, stopping for a long second before racing hard and heavy in my chest.

There was a man in my store.

I grabbed a garden hoe from the exceptionally handy long-handled tools display to my right and took a couple of slow, quiet steps in his direction. Readying myself for a fight I really didn't want to have. Elmer followed me, not growling or barking or protecting us in any way. He really must have been angry about the mask I'd strapped on him.

Lesson learned—don't piss off the dog if you wanted him to act as your guard.

Four steps, two deep breaths, and a quick prayer to whatever deity might listen, and I was ready. To do what, I didn't know, but I started with a firmly spoken question. "What are you doing in here?"

The man spun, dropping the items he'd apparently been holding—two water supply lines and a wax ring. Someone was replacing a toilet.

"Sorry," the guy said, shooting me a sincerely uncomfortable smile. "I'm Mike from Value Hardware Cooperative. I'd heard someone was going to reopen the store, and I wanted to stop by to see if there was anything I could do to help. This spot used to be on my route."

Route. Value Hardware. Mike. As in Mike Allen, delivery driver for the wholesaler Rose had used and another one of the suspects on my list of people who might be stealing from the manor. His breaking in was awfully convenient. Weird and seriously scary, but convenient.

I held on to my hoe, though. "Nice to meet you, Mike. Aunt Gwendolyn has told me a bit about you."

His smile turned more authentic. "She's a real nice lady, as was Miss Rose. I've missed them both."

Enough to steal from them? Possibly. Considering what he'd dropped, likely. I nodded toward the forgotten plumbing repair items at his feet. "You planning on replacing a toilet?"

"Yeah, totally. I bought a new house and want to put a chair-height toilet in my half bath. Can't go full ADA because I don't have the room for an elongated bowl, you know?" He glanced down, looking surprised. As if he had no idea how those items had ended up right in front of him. "I was totally going to pay for those."

"Oh yeah?" I finally lowered my weapon, mostly to scratch at the itch that suddenly attacked my wrist. So many untruths in Reverie Springs. I really needed to get my hands on some Benadryl if I was going to stay put in this town. "Because we're closed and have no point-of-sale system in place, so that might prove to be a challenge. How'd you get in here, anyway?"

"I have a key."

That...wasn't good. "You have a key. To this store."

"Yeah. Miss Rose gave it to me when I was delivering for her in case I came when she was busy with customers."

I could have asked for it back, but being in the hardware business, I knew how easy it was to make extra copies of keys. Thankfully, I also knew how to rekey a door, replace a lock, and—when necessary—call a locksmith. Mike's access was about to be revoked; he just didn't know it. Didn't need to either.

I leaned on the hoe, trying hard to look casual even though my heart pounded in a very non-casual way. "So, Mike, tell me about this house you bought. You said it was new—as in new construction?"

"Oh no. Not at all. In fact, it's a historic home on the edge of town. Have you ever heard of—"

"Mikey has come for a visit!" Aunt Gwendolyn flew into the store like some sort of exotic, smoke-colored, and very loud bird. Today's outfit consisted of another gravity defying skirt in swirls of gray and black that made her look like a wraith flying over the earth as it burned. Totally fitting "How are you, my dear?"

Mike grinned, his entire face lighting up as he looked her way. "I'm good, Miss Gwen. Real good."

"Excellent." Gwendolyn stopped beside me, staying close enough to touch shoulders. "I see you've met my great-niece, Brylie."

"Brylie." Mike turned my way once more. "We were just getting acquainted."

"Good, that's good. Oh." Aunt Gwendolyn lunged forward, grabbing the supply lines and wax gasket box off the floor before holding them out to Mike. "Seems like you dropped these."

"Yes, ma'am." Mike's cheeks darkened, his neck flushing right along with them. "Sorry. I got distracted by shopping while I was waiting for someone to arrive. I'll pay for those."

I opened my mouth, but Aunt Gwendolyn grabbed my wrist—the seriously itchy one—and held fast. Quieting me.

"I won't hear of it. You take those with you. Rose would have been thrilled to be able to help you with your new house." Aunt Gwendolyn patted my wrist, shooting me a sly smile before leaving me behind to walk with Mike. Physically guiding the man toward the back of the store. "So, have you started working on your landscaping yet? There are some lovely hostas at the manor that we could split for you in the fall if you'd like."

"I didn't know there were hostas there. I'd only ever seen the flowers."

"Of course. Right by the back door off the dining room. You've been back there, right?"

Mike shook his head, following along as my sneaky great-aunt dug for information in the politest way possible.

"I've never seen the back of the house. That one time I came by to see you and Miss Rose, I came through the front."

I stayed behind them, trying hard to figure out if he was telling the truth or not. He seemed sincere enough, but he could be an adept liar. Or I could be a really bad judge of character. I wasn't itching, so that had to mean something. Right?

"Oh, and Brylie?"

I jerked, staring at my aunt, who looked about ready to laugh. "Yeah?"

"Nice mask. Though you might want to take it off when chatting with customers. It's very distracting."

I dragged the breathing mask—the one I'd totally forgotten about—off my face. "Good call."

Mike tried hard, he really did, but a slight chuckle escaped him anyway. "Looks like your dog beat you to it."

I glanced behind me, finding a sleeping Elmer curled up by one of the outdoor lighting endcaps, the mask I'd worked so hard to adjust just for him hanging from his neck like some sort of absurd ID tag.

Outsmarted by my own Basset hound.

Figures.

Later that night, I took a demasked Elmer for another stroll down Main Street. We'd spent the entire afternoon in the store —cleaning, sorting, trashing, and reorganizing the garden department. I had to admit, I was tired from all the lifting and my back was still screaming about the fact that I had been sleeping in my van along with performing all the physical work, but the store was looking much better since I'd started. My exhaustion had been well earned.

As I made my way back to the hardware store, I spotted Mike Allen walking across the street. He headed straight into Ander's diner, not noticing me three storefronts down. As much as eating dinner in the only restaurant in town seemed like a very normal thing to do, I'd been eating breakfast and lunch there every day and hadn't run into him. Tonight must have been special in some way to change his habits, more special than just the fact that it was one of the few nights Ander opened for the dinner crowd.

I couldn't help myself—I had to know who he was meeting for dinner or if he planned to eat alone. I mean, it couldn't hurt to walk by, right? The streets were shadowy, and the diner was still well-lit enough to peer inside without too many people noticing. A quick look was all I wanted.

So I crept. And I kept my steps super slow. And I whispered soft words of encouragement to Elmer to make sure he knew we weren't stopping and this wasn't nap time. At least until I made it to the corner of the diner windows, where I paused long enough to get a good look inside.

Surprise, surprise. Mike sat at a back table with a pretty

blonde who looked to be about the same age as him. Perhaps a girlfriend or a date. Totally normal.

What stood out as not normal, though, was the couple closer to the window. There was a large, dark-haired man sitting at a table with Joan—Rose's sister and hater of unleashed pets. Who he was and how they knew each other, I'd have to ask Aunt Gwendolyn, though the fact that she was obviously at least friendly with a man that size did move Joan back into contention for possible thief. With someone like that helping her, the physicality of taking the missing fireplace mantel seemed way more possible. If only I could hear what they were saying...

"What are you doing out here?"

I spun, nearly tripping over Elmer in my hurry not to be murdered by someone surprising me from behind. Ander stood between me and the street, frowning. Likely not wanting to murder me.

But his expression definitely wasn't a happy one—Grumpy was back.

"Sorry. I was just..." Spying on Joan and her dinner partner like some sort of creeper. No way would that go over well. "How are you out here and not in there cooking?"

He grunted. "I have a line cook for dinner service. I needed to run an errand that couldn't wait, so. I left him in charge. Now your turn—what are you doing?"

Might as well go with the truth. "Snooping and giving Elmer a break while I figure out what I want for dinner."

"Hamburger, medium, with sautéed mushrooms and blue cheese sauce served with sweet potato waffle fries."

Well, now I'm drooling. "What?"

"It's the special today. You mentioned once that you liked

mushrooms and blue cheese on your burgers, so I played with a few recipes and came up with one."

Joan, Mike, and the dark-haired man...forgotten. "You made a special burger because of me?"

His face, the shock there—totally unexpected. "No. Of course not. I just thought if you liked them, others might as well."

"Ah, got it." I scratched at my itchy palm, the irritation a reminder that I still hadn't made it to a drug store for some antihistamine. Also a good indicator that the man was lying—not that I was going to call him out on it. I may have been winning at hardware store revamp, but I was failing at the whole taking care of myself and minding my own business thing. Besides, this seemed like a good sort of lie. One that made me feel all warm and giddy inside.

Ander could lie about paying attention to me all he wanted so long as he kept paying attention.

But the cantankerous chef was far more observant than I gave him credit for. "So, are you coming inside, or do you want to stay out here to keep an eye on Mike some more?"

I darted a look his way, unable to stop my mouth from opening and spilling all my secrets. "How did you know?"

He shrugged, staring past me and into the restaurant. "Lots of women look his way. It seemed a logical choice."

"Oh, no. I'm not—it's not like that."

"Sure." He turned as if to leave. "Come in for a burger, Brylie. I'll make Elmer some eggs for dinner."

"Ander, wait." I stepped toward him, my gut twisting in something close to desperation. "Seriously, I'm not watching Mike for romantic reasons. More nefarious ones."

The man stopped, furrowing his brow. "Planning on kidnapping him?"

"What? No. Of course not."

"Good, because I'd really hate to have to deal with the sheriff again."

Him and me both. "That's sort of my problem. Someone has been breaking in to Willow Manor and taking things—knobs, photos, doors, a mantel. Aunt Gwendolyn and I made a list of people who might steal from her since she was pretty adamant no one would steal from Miss Rose. Joan is on the list, as is Mike. Aunt Gwen thinks the sheriff is too inept to handle this, so we're investigating people ourselves. Quietly. And without any sort of knowledge of how to do it."

He grunted, looking highly doubtful and probably reconsidering calling the sheriff.

Or maybe not. "Joan can be a handful for sure, though I never pegged her for the thieving sort. Mike seems like a nice enough guy, but I don't know him well enough to say if he might be trouble or not. Either way, if you think he might be stealing from Miss Gwen, I'll help you keep an eye on him."

I could have been knocked over with a feather. "Really?"

"Of course. I only moved back here about seven years ago, and Miss Rose and Miss Gwen were the first to welcome me home. Miss Rose helped me design the interior of the diner and sold me a lot of the stuff I needed to rehab the space at cost, too. I owe them both."

"I appreciate that. Aunt Gwendolyn seemed really heartbroken over all the things missing from the manor."

"She and Miss Rose loved that old house—the whole town knew it. I can see why someone stealing from the place would be so shocking."

"Yeah. I just want to restore the house to what it should be. It seems important to her." And to me, apparently. My stomach clenched, my eyes burning with unshed tears. I wasn't a crier by nature, so the overall sensation of sadness that had appeared out of nowhere took me by complete surprise.

"You okay, Brylie?"

Swallowing hard, trying to hold back the wave of emotion pushing me in weird directions, I nodded toward the door of the diner and ignored his question completely. "I should probably try that burger for dinner. Since you made it because of my preferences and all."

Ander nodded, not pushing me on...well, anything. Watching me with an intense expression but not speaking or expecting me to fill the silence. Something I appreciated. Words could be hard.

Finally, he sighed. "Give me a minute."

He jogged to the truck parked on the street, hopping up into the bed where a few large black metal things rested. Metal things that looked like—

"Tables!" I hurried forward, helping him unload the two iron bistro sets. "You're putting in tables for alfresco dining, aren't you?"

He jumped down to the sidewalk, rubbing the back of his neck as he looked at the black metal pieces. "Yeah, well—it seemed like a good idea."

One I'd commented about. Just like the burger. The man really did pay attention to me. "It is, and I, for one, am thrilled at the idea of sitting outside on a night like tonight and eating my dinner."

"Let me get them set up, and you can do just that." He lugged the heavy pieces to the space under the awning over the windows, even sliding the water bowl he put out every day closer so my dog could move as little as possible once I sat down. He understood the laziness of Elmer.

"This is amazing." I took a seat, grinning up at him. "I've

got some awesome string lights you can put up in the canopy of the awning—it would give this space a nice, romantic glow."

"I don't know about all that." Ander took a step back, frowning once more. "I'd better get back to work so I can make your burger. Enjoy the new tables."

"Thanks, I'm sure I will."

And with that, he strolled inside while I settled in to enjoy a little time outside. Burgers and tables and eggs for Elmer—seriously, the man didn't miss a thing. Having him on my side keeping an eye on the suspects might be the best idea ever.

Joan and the dark-haired man walked out a few minutes after I sat down, totally missing me sitting in the shadows of the awning and striding in the direction of the hardware store. Not that it mattered—the store was closed and the lights were off.

I'd also changed the locks.

No more surprise visits from anyone. At least not at the store.

The manor...well, that could be a different story.

Chapter Nine

I couldn't tell which would be the death of me—the dilapidated hardware store or the house. But after two weeks of working every day on each, I was done. Cooked. Exhausted to the point of losing my grip on reality. Either that, or the house was trying to mess with my mind.

"This is getting ridiculous," I said as I slammed the powder room door closed for what had to be the fifteenth time in the past few hours. "There is nothing wrong with this handle. Why does the door keep falling open?"

Elmer—the only other living being in the house that I knew of—didn't answer me. He simply snored from his favorite napping spot at the bottom of the stairs. Me, I stared at the door in question and waited. There was no reason for that darn door to open on its own, and yet it did. All the time. Not when I was around, but if I closed it and walked away, I'd come back to it being wide open.

Also driving me mad were the leaks—every now and again, I'd turn a corner and spot a small puddle. Nothing like when I first came to the house, but enough to worry me. I was in the middle of pulling up the warped floorboards and replacing them with some of the extras I'd found stored in the building I had to assume had been once used as a garage. If I had enough wood, I could repair the floor and really kick-start bringing the foyer back to life.

But not if the house kept leaking on me.

"Okay," I said, still watching the door. Knowing it would open again as soon as I turned my back on it. "I want to finish the porch, which means prepping the door for paint. Please just...stay closed. I don't need sawdust gumming up the sink in there."

Not that I should be talking to a house, but at that point, it seemed to be my only option.

Accepting the fact that my world had become a vastly different place since moving to Reverie Springs—I'd never talked to a house in California, that was for sure—I grabbed my toolbox and got to work.

The front door was a solid piece of wood, heavy and strong and obviously old. The window inset had wavy seed glass with lead carving out small and large rectangles around the edges, giving the whole thing a decidedly antique feel. It was truly lovely, though it had obviously not weathered well. That was okay—a wooden door was easy enough to repair. A little sanding, some solid prep work, and a couple coats of paint would bring her back to her full glory and finish my porch restoration. Not that much had needed restoring—the narrow but long space had really only required some deep cleaning. I'd replaced the outside light bulbs, polished the fixtures, and cleaned all the front windows. The house looked welcoming, if not a little overgrown. That was okay, though. I'd dive into the window boxes and flower beds in the fall when planting made more sense. Next up was the door, then the floors, then repairing the fallen wallpaper. So much work, but I had a feeling it would be worth it once completed.

I had just finished filling in a few of the deeper gouges on the door when a truck pulled into the drive. It looked familiar, as did the bearded man driving it and the woman riding beside him.

"Aunt Gwendolyn?" I hopped off the porch, hurrying to the passenger side, suddenly self-conscious about my ratty shorts and threadbare tank. "What are you doing out here?"

Aunt Gwendolyn stepped down from the truck, her silver braid swaying and nearly matching the gray color of her sundress. "I was telling Ander how hard you'd been working and how worried I'd been about you, and he offered to drive me out here to check on you."

The man in question slipped around the front of the truck, watching me cautiously. "She was adamant that you needed a good meal and a break from all the work."

I mean...I couldn't even begin to argue that point. "I don't have much here in the way of food if you're expecting lunch."

"Oh, my silly niece." Gwen swatted my arm, opening the back door to the crew cab truck. "As if I'd show up empty-handed."

She tugged a large picnic basket out of the back, stepping to the side with a smile when Ander grabbed it from her. They'd come to visit *and* brought me food. Nicest people ever.

"I don't have the dining room set up, but I did get the back deck cleared off and set up some patio furniture I found. It could be a nice place to eat."

Ander nodded toward the door. "Lead the way."

I did as I was told, holding on to Aunt Gwendolyn's arm as we walked into the house and down the hallway. She didn't pause, didn't stumble or gasp or look shaken this time. She almost looked...happy. As if seeing the house in the shambles of my repairs was better than what she'd walked into the first time. And perhaps it was—a house being restored was a good sort of messy. There was life to a remodel.

But as we passed across the soon-to-be-repaired floors, I couldn't help but look to the side. The bathroom door stood open again, making me frown. And cuss a little under my breath.

"Something wrong?" Aunt Gwendolyn asked.

"Not really. I just can't keep that bathroom door closed." The floor groaned loudly as I took my next step, and a creaking sort of noise sounded from within the walls.

Aunt Gwendolyn simply smiled through the sudden symphony of the old house settling. "Doors aren't meant to be closed all the time. Rooms need attention, too."

Of course they did.

Ander followed us down the hallway, his steps causing just as many squeaks and groans as ours, while carrying the picnic basket and looking around. The wallpaper still hung in strips instead of clinging to the walls and some of the pictures were definitely in need of a good scrubbing, but the windows were clean and bright, so natural light shone through the space. Plus, there wasn't an inch of water to walk through. I considered that a definite improvement. Noisy but dry—I'd take it.

Once on the back deck, Ander jumped right into setting up the table with all of the food, plates, and utensils he'd brought. There were even serving spoons, which meant I didn't need to lift a finger for this meal. Bless him.

"Join us," Aunt Gwendolyn said to Ander once we were ready to serve. "You should enjoy the meal you brought."

Ander sat down across from me, spooning piles of salad into individual bowls before pulling out a mason jar filled with his famous candied nuts. Which he pushed across the table to me. Smart man.

"Thank you for all of this."

He shrugged. "No problem."

But it was a problem—he didn't have a lot of help at the restaurant, and it was only closed one day during the week. To take his personal time to cook me food and drive all the way out to the manor was a lot. I needed to make sure he understood how much I appreciated the effort. Somehow.

"I walked past the store last night," Ander said, focusing those dark eyes on me. "How much longer until you think you'll be open?"

My heart stumbled, pausing for a moment before pounding in my chest. "Another few weeks. I have so much to do between the house and the store and getting inventory in."

"Her father owned a hardware store," Aunt Gwendolyn said with a smile. "She's going to be great at running the place because she's already done it. For her dad. Right, Brylie?"

Grief was a funny thing. I could go days without being sad about losing my dad, without missing him. And then, out of the blue, I'd be sinking back down into the well of loss and loneliness his death caused.

This was more like being thrown down that well, but still. Thinking about my dad hurt. A lot.

"Right," I said with a slow nod. "The retail hardware business is pretty much all I know."

Ander caught my eye, his deep, penetrating gaze practically absorbing me. Soaking me into his warmth and care. He didn't push for more info, though. Just gave me a single head bob and said, "If there's anything I can do to help, you let me know. Okay?"

No itchiness. No lies detected. I nodded in response and let my gaze fall back to my salad.

"So," Aunt Gwen said in between bites and making the most obvious subject change ever. "Any updates on the Mike situation?"

Ander sat back, placing his napkin on the table and giving her an intense look. "He's been into the restaurant a couple times. Twice with a blond woman, once all alone. He doesn't usually come in, so three times in two weeks is excessive for him. Otherwise, all seems normal."

She looked at me, as if I might have more to add.

I did not. "I've had no issues at the store or out here."

Aunt Gwen picked at her food, frowning. "Maybe they've given up—realized things couldn't be taken so easily and will now leave the manor alone."

I met Ander's gaze, pushing aside the emotions I felt in meeting his eyes. He carried the same sort of disbelieving expression I would have bet I was wearing. No one forgot free money. They'd be back. It would only be a matter of time.

After lunch, as Ander packed away his dishes and serving ware, Aunt Gwendolyn opened her purse and reminded me why Reverie Springs was just so odd.

"Here you go, dear." She handed me a bottle with a watery, dark liquid inside of it. "Take this."

I was almost too afraid to ask. "What is it?"

"A potion to help you sleep. You've been looking tired."

A potion. Hexes and potions. All brewed over my hardware store. Here's to hoping this one didn't smell as bad as her hexes. "What's in it?"

"A witch never reveals her secrets." She stood from the table, moving slower than I would have expected. Looking almost stiff. "I'll just use the powder room, then perhaps we can head back to town. Does that sound okay, Ander?"

The big man stopped himself from frowning but definitely showed his concern in that furrowed brow and stiff top lip. "Whatever you like. This trip was your idea—I'm just the chauffeur."

"Such a nice man." She patted him on the arm, shooting me a wink at the same time. "And single. I don't know how that can be. The local women must be clueless."

Ander huffed a laugh, both of us watching the old woman traipse into the house as if she hadn't just dropped the biggest hint in the history of the world on us. Sneaky, sneaky.

"I don't think women are clueless," he said, sounding far more agitated than I would have expected.

"It's okay. Old women love to play matchmaker sometimes." I took a final sip of the water I'd been drinking, twirling the empty glass in my hands once finished. "Though it is surprising that you're single. You seem really...nice."

He huffed...again. "Maybe that's my problem."

"What is?"

"Being nice. Nice is the kiss of death in dating, according to my sister."

I stood, frowning. His sister was definitely wrong. "No, it's not."

"Yes, it is."

"Why would it be a bad thing to be nice?"

"My sister claims being nice is a weakness."

And suddenly, I hated his sister. "Well, she's wrong. Completely. I would never think of you as weak."

He nodded, his voice softening as he asked a simple, "No?"

"No." I reached out and grabbed his forearm. "Sorry for being so blunt, but your sister's an idiot."

He laughed, the sound raucous and rowdy in the quiet of the house. "Veterinarian degree aside."

"Totally." I rose to my feet and grabbed my plate, heading inside. Looking over my shoulder to find Ander following me. "You said she wasn't local—where does she live?"

His face hardened, his attitude darkening. Grumpy slipping back into place. "Tennessee."

Conversation...over. I set the plate on the counter and turned, suddenly far more nervous than I had been with the man. Acutely aware that we were alone in my kitchen. "That's nice. Tennessee, I mean. I guess. I've never actually—"

Suddenly, Ander stood before me. Practically against me. Crowding me with his body and stealing all the oxygen from the world. My heart thudded and my breath caught at how much room he took up. At how daringly he blasted through my personal comfort zone and inserted himself in my space. But my goodness, did the man smell good.

"What are you doing?" I asked, suddenly unsure what to do with my hands. Leave them by my sides, grab hold of him with them, clasp them around the glass still dangling from my fingers? I was lost—completely blindsided by the presence of this man in this moment. And I think I liked it.

"Do you want me to be nice to you, Brylie?"

I...had no idea how to answer that question. "Maybe."

He grunted, staring down at me. Wrapping me in a blanket of emotions that swirled and collided like storm clouds. Like the start of a tornado on an otherwise uneventful day, bringing the scent of ozone and rain with him. Brightening my personal sky with the lightning bolts in his stare. The man was dangerous...in the best possible way. And just as sneaky as Aunt Gwendolyn—how had he been hiding all of *this* from me?

"You let me know when that maybe firms up to a yes, then we'll talk." Another breath, another inch closer, a light brushing of his hand against mine as he took the glass I was still holding, and then...nothing. He backed away, set the glass on the counter behind me, and headed outside, leaving me standing in the kitchen, in the fading light of the late afternoon, holding my chest and trying hard to catch my breath. To figure out which way was up after that encounter. Goodness me, that man had given me one heck of a tease.

I *definitely* liked it.

"Not tonight," I whispered to myself as I shook out my hair and took a deep breath. "Another time, but not tonight."

Because I had a lot on my plate, and starting something with the local diner owner would only add to that. But maybe, once I had the store opened and the house in a livable condition. Maybe.

"You don't forget to take that potion," Aunt Gwendolyn said as I helped her into the truck just a few minutes later. After I'd calmed down enough to not want to jump into Ander's arms. Or throw something at him. "I want you well rested."

"I'll take it." What I didn't say was that I was tired because I was still sleeping in my van. No one wanted to admit they were too afraid of an empty house to stay in it, especially not me. Besides, what they didn't know wouldn't hurt them. "Drive safe now."

Ander gave me a serious sort of smile before handing me a slip of paper, his long fingers brushing mine. "Here. In case you need me."

For what, he didn't specify, but I certainly wasn't going to ask him to explain. Especially not in front of Aunt Gwendolyn. Still, I looked over the paper, and my heart did a little jump. There were ten digits scribbled in an aggressive and sharp sort of handwriting—a phone number. Ander's phone number.

"Is this for the phone at the diner?"

"No. That's just for my sister and customers. This is my cell."

"Oh." Which meant I should probably give him my number as well. It would only be polite, right? "There's not a lot of service out here to send a text, especially out front, but I can tell you mine."

"Absolutely." He typed on his screen while I spoke the numbers I knew by heart before setting his device into a holder on his dashboard. "Ready, Miss Gwen?"

"Ready." She reached out to cup my cheek. "The porch and entry look lovely already. You're doing such a good job. Rose would approve. Sleep well, dear one."

Rose would approve. Something about that compliment, about that wording, settled something that had been irritating my soul. It made all the work and effort worthwhile, made me think that I was doing what was right.

Made me happy she'd come by.

I watched the truck pull out of the drive, crossing my arms over my chest and trying my darnedest not to give weight to the crushing sense of loneliness their departure left behind. I was fine—I had the house, Elmer, and would get a good night's sleep with Aunt Gwendolyn's potion. That was really all I needed in that moment. Or so I told myself.

But before I could sleep, there was more work to be done.

"Okay, door. It's just you and me." And a snoring Basset hound, but he wouldn't mind being excluded from the conversation.

Three hours and more sanding than any person should have to do to a single door later, I had locked up the house and retreated to my van. My arms were on fire and my back positively ached, but I was happy with the results. I'd filled in every crack and gouge, sanded the entire surface to smooth the damage, and given the hinges a good greasing. I still needed to paint the door, but it was definitely ready for a couple coats of a quality exterior paint and maybe a new lockset to dress it up. Something antique and showy.

Something Rose might have loved.

I crawled into the van, giving my lazy dog time to follow me. Elmer snuggled into his spot, sighing and beginning to snore before I even closed the door. Typical.

I should have gone straight to sleep—especially with how tired I felt—but I wasn't quite ready to surrender to the day. Instead, I sat in the van, looking over the house as the moonlight bathed it in a soft glow, doing my best to see it as something more than a burden. Deep down, I knew I was tired and overworked, but there had been moments over the past few weeks when I had simply been ungrateful for what I'd been given. In that moment, with the waning moon barely visible in the night sky, I felt nothing *but* grateful. I had been blessed with an opportunity most people would never receive, and I felt awful for not appreciating it more.

"To a good night's sleep," I said to my snoring dog, raising the potion bottle as if to toast. Trusting my wild great-aunt was being honest when she'd said this was nothing more than a drink for better sleep. "And to remembering how lucky I am even when things go wrong."

A lesson I definitely needed reminding about.

And so, I drank. The potion tasted sweet, the liquid thicker than I would have expected but not bad. I finished the entire bottle before rolling into the back and tugging my blanket over me. Maybe, just maybe, I'd start sleeping inside soon. Maybe. If

I could figure out who had been breaking in and get them to stop. Then I'd feel better. Then I could rest easy.

I needed to focus more on that issue.

Tomorrow. I'd start tomorrow.

And I remembered nothing after that thought.

Chapter Ten

As with all my mornings the past few weeks, Elmer woke me up with a sharp bark. There was only one problem I noticed when I opened my eyes—it wasn't morning. He wasn't trying to keep us from cooking inside the van while the hot sun shone down on us. In fact, the sun hadn't even begun its ascent in the sky. The world was dark, the land around us quiet, and the day not yet begun. But Elmer barked again. And again. And then he started to growl.

Code word: emergency.

I jumped up from the back seat, my back twinging as I did. The pain didn't stop me, though. Elmer loved his sleep far too much to bark over nothing. Especially not in the middle of the night. He was warning me about something.

I hushed the howling Basset hound and looked outside, giving my eyes a second to adjust to being open, wishing my brain would catch up as well. It didn't take long to spot the issue, to be honest. That issue being a human figure creeping through the back fields toward the house.

I should have stayed in the van, should have started the

engine and gotten out of there as fast as possible. But this was my house, and I was repairing it in a way that Rose would have approved of and that made Aunt Gwendolyn happy. The shadowy figure in the field was not running me off my land.

"Time to fight, Elmer."

The dog didn't respond, though he did wag his tail. Just once, but I understood his message loud and clear. He was ready to go to war.

I waited until the person cleared the corner of the conservatory and disappeared behind it before diving out the side door. My legs pumped and my breaths came fast as I raced to the front door, unlocking it with ease and hurrying inside. Elmer followed right on my heels.

"Good boy," I whispered before shutting the door and engaging the lock. Thank goodness I hadn't decided to leave the dead bolt off the wood surface to make painting easier.

With the dog following me, I hurried through the house, keeping my ears open for any sounds of an intruder. The house sat quiet—really quiet. Even the floors weren't squeaking under my feet. It was as if the structure itself were holding its breath right along with me.

"We all need to breathe," I whispered, taking a deep breath myself. "We'll be okay. I'll get us help."

As soon as I hit the kitchen, I pulled my phone out of my pocket and prayed for better signal inside the house than outside it. A single bar glowed in the corner of the screen, indicating I at least had some sort of service. That bar was going to have to be better than nothing. I probably should have called Aunt Gwen or the sheriff, should have dialed 911 to have the police come running. Instead, I pulled up the first person in my contacts who came to mind and tapped to dial. It took a long time for the phone to connect to anything, but it did. Finally.

Ander answered on the second ring, sounding sleepy and slightly startled. "Brylie?"

"I'm so sorry to call," I said, keeping my voice down, the lights off, and my eyes on the conservatory windows as I watched for shadows that shouldn't be there. "I know this isn't really your thing, but I need some help."

"What's wrong?" he asked, suddenly sounding much more awake.

"There's someone outside creeping toward the house."

"Get upstairs and lock yourself in a bathroom. I'm on my way."

"Yeah, okay. Just...text me when you get here so I know to open the door."

"I'll text you. Be safe."

As if I had an option there. I didn't see any reason to go upstairs—if someone was breaking in, I wanted to know who it was and what they were stealing from me—but locking myself in a room seemed like a solidly good idea. I chose the powder room off the main hallway, the one with the door that wouldn't stay closed. I took Elmer with me and locked us inside, hoping against hope that this time, the door wouldn't pop open on its own.

"Come on, house. Keep us safe."

For several minutes, that door stayed perfectly still. Locked into place the way it should have been. It stayed closed enough for whoever was outside to apparently decide the front door would be easier to break in to than any of the ones along the back. How did I know that? One second, everything was silent, and the next, I heard the telltale sound of someone jiggling the front door handle. The one I'd reattached somewhat loosely after all the sanding, simply to be able to lock up the house. I would have said it could have been Ander, but he'd promised he'd text when he got to the house, and he hadn't.

Intruder alert, for sure.

I was about to sneak out into the hall, to creep toward the door to look outside, when Elmer started barking once more. The handle jiggling stopped, and the bathroom door popped open as if someone had turned the handle and pushed their way inside. Thankfully though, the hall stood empty. The door had simply...unlatched itself.

Impossible, and yet I'd just seen it with my own eyes. Something inside me, some sort of instinct, told me to move. And with the door open, the house seemed to agree with that option. Time to go.

I had taken just two steps into the foyer, hadn't even cleared the stairs overhead that created the end of the hallway, when my phone rang.

Ander.

"Yeah," I said as soon as I swiped to connect the call.

"I'm parking now. Let me in."

I didn't answer him, didn't even keep the call connected. I tapped to end it and rushed to the door, unlatching the dead bolt and swinging it wide. Revealing a man on the porch.

It wasn't Ander standing before me.

My scream had Elmer howling, and I nearly fell over the dog as he rushed past me. Full-on Basset hound protection mode activated. Not that he needed to do much. Ander suddenly appeared beside the strange man, grabbing him and taking him to the ground so quickly, I almost thought I'd imagined it.

The guy was definitely facedown on my porch, though.

No imagining there.

"What are you doing here?" Ander asked, holding the other man down like some sort of wrestler.

The man held his hands over his head, looking like someone surrendering to the police. "I'm sorry—it's me. Thomas."

Ander glanced up at me—a feeling of confusion and rage setting my nerves alight—before crawling off the man and helping him to his feet.

"Thomas?" Ander tugged back the hoodie covering the man's head, exposing a face that looked really familiar to me. "Why are you here in the middle of the night?"

The man—Thomas, apparently—kept his hands up and took a step back. Away from me. "I thought I saw someone out in my fields. I was coming to investigate when I noticed them moving toward the house. I was just checking to make sure everything was okay over here."

Ander looked my way, still breathing hard. "This the guy you saw creeping toward the house?"

"I don't know—it was really dark, and the person was far... Wait, you're the guy with Joan."

Thomas frowned and cocked his head. "I don't have anyone with me."

I shook my head, that dark hair and face striking every bell of memory I had. "No, no. I mean, I've seen you a few times with Joan."

"Oh, yeah," he said, nodding. "Ms. Turlington planted a good-sized garden this year, and she's been asking me for tips."

"Gardening tips?"

"Right. Soil amendments, companion plants, fertilizers... that sort of stuff."

"Huh." Joan didn't seem like the type to get her hands dirty to me—unless there was a bottle buried in that garden plot—but I didn't feel a single itch. He wasn't lying. "So, you think there was someone else outside?"

"There was definitely another man out here," Thomas said. "I swear it."

"A man?" Ander asked. "Are you sure it was a man and not a woman?"

"Well...no. Not really. I just assumed..." Thomas trailed off, looking a bit confused. Not that I could blame him.

"I couldn't tell if it was a man or a woman either," I said. "They were just too far away."

"See? She couldn't tell either," Thomas said.

But Ander didn't seem convinced, which made me doubt as well. Except for the fact that I wasn't the least bit itchy.

I sighed. "He's not lying."

Ander gave me a confused look. "How do you know?"

How to explain to someone I'd basically just met that lies made me itch? Yeah...that'd be well received. "I just do. There was someone else in the fields."

Thomas glanced from me to Ander and back, relaxing his arms and looking decidedly less nervous. "I was going to check all the doors and windows on the house to make sure they were locked since I knew Miss Gwen's niece was staying out here. I swear—that was all I was doing."

Still no itching, which just solidified my opinion of him as a non-liar. My senses weren't always totally accurate, my intuition a little off now and again, but I was pretty confident this time. "Thanks for trying to help. Whoever was out there definitely scared me."

"Me too." He held out a hand. "Name's Thomas Lee. I've been renting the fields of the manor to do my farming since before Miss Rose bought the place."

He was also one of the four suspects in the break-ins at the manor. A position I suddenly had doubts about. "I'm Brylie Scott. The new owner of Willow Manor."

"I hope we can continue working together. The field rentals have always been a real boon to me and given the manor owner some extra pocket money. Unless you were thinking of farming them yourself."

I laughed. Out loud. Because that idea was super funny. "Oh gosh, no. Farming is definitely not in my wheelhouse. I'd rather see someone else using the fields than try to do any of that stuff myself."

The man smiled. "Best to leave the farming to the professionals if it's not in your blood. Between the equipment and the chemicals, it's not the safest of jobs around."

True. And also a good reminder. "Just so you know, I have a dog."

Thomas frowned and sent an intentional look Elmer's way. "Yeah. I know."

"Chemicals," I said, stumbling to make myself clear. "If you're using chemicals out there, either they need to be pet-friendly or I need to know when to keep my dog under watch."

"Of course," Thomas said. "I prefer not to use a lot of insecticides, though I do use some fertilizers. I'll let you know when it's time so you can maybe keep the pup on a leash."

What was it with this town and their leashes? "I won't need to go that far—the dog barely leaves my side, let alone goes running into a field. I just want to keep him as far away from all that as possible."

"Understood. I'll take care with the products I use." Thomas nodded at a very taciturn-looking Ander. "Well, it seems all is okay here. I'll be heading home. You keep an eye out for visitors, Brylie. I'm not too far away if you need help."

"Thanks, Thomas. I appreciate it." Appreciated it but

didn't go out of my way to give him my number or take his. I may not have thought him a liar, but that didn't mean I fully trusted him yet. Unlike the other man at my side.

"You okay?" Ander asked after Thomas had once again disappeared into the night.

I shut the front door, engaging the dead bolt just to be safe. Trying my best to ignore the way my hand shook as I pulled it back. "Yeah. Fine."

But Ander was not a stupid man. "You don't have to lie to me."

"I'm not..." But the words wouldn't come. Instead, I began to shake all over. To tremble from the bottom of my feet to my shoulders as the adrenaline I'd been running on suddenly dropped. Ander didn't miss a beat, though. He grabbed me and tugged me close, wrapping his arms around me in a hold that was both calming and inciting, that rocked me right down to my soul. That held me together in a moment when I was ready to fall to pieces. Ander's arms felt good. Way too good. And so very safe.

I could only hold on to him even tighter. "Ander."

"It'll be okay. We'll figure out who keeps showing up here, and we'll get them sent to jail. Then everything will be fine."

I didn't itch, but I certainly didn't believe him. How would we find the person? And when? Because I still wasn't sleeping in the house, and I wasn't sure how much longer I could get away with that.

Ander yawned, breaking my concentration and making me feel like a real jerk for thinking only of myself. "You're tired. Why don't you go on home? I'll be fine."

Did my skin itch at my own lie? Yes. Yes, it did. My inner wrist particularly, if you wanted to know. Because I was about as far from fine as I'd ever been.

And Ander knew that. "Me leaving is not happening. You have to have a couch around here somewhere."

I did in what I had deemed the family room of the house, so I led him down the hall and into the space. A huge, stone fireplace dominated the one wall, custom white bookshelves finishing off that length and lending a certain softness to the room. Once I fixed it up, maybe gave it a good painting, the room would be ready for new furniture and a big television. And books. Lots of books. I almost couldn't wait. But for now, I had a few pieces left behind by Aunt Gwendolyn and an awful lot of dust.

"Sit with me," Ander said, tugging me onto the dirty sectional that took up most of the floor space. "I just want to stay with you until dawn, then I'll leave. Nothing bad ever happens when the sun is up."

He was dead wrong about that, but I was too tired to argue so I sat down beside him and kept my mouth shut.

The dark room did nothing to help keep me awake, though. It didn't seem to help Ander either, because within a matter of minutes, his breath had evened out and he appeared to be asleep. Next to me. Such a sight, that man leaning against the couch with his head back and his eyes closed. One I was thankful to witness.

After a few minutes of definite almost-snoring, I gave Ander a little nudge to see if he was really out before rising to my feet and sneaking into the linen closet upstairs. All the blankets I'd used to clean up the water were folded neatly on the shelves, laundered and ready for new jobs. Handy. I grabbed one and headed back downstairs, laying the fabric over Ander so he wouldn't grow cold. And then I sat at his feet, and I watched the sky outside begin to lighten. And I didn't fall asleep.

Instead, I listened to the settling noises of the house, and I worried. A lot. About everything—the house, the intruder, the store, how much work the place would require so I didn't fail, how I had nowhere else to go if I did.

I sat and I stewed and I tried really hard not to feel overwhelmed. Tried and failed at that one, for sure.

Eventually, Elmer climbed into my lap as if sensing my unease. "We're good, boy. It's going to be good."

The house groaned, the sound oddly comforting in the dark. As was Elmer's substantial weight on my thighs. And the sound of Ander breathing from behind me.

Such a noisy night, and yet so soothing.

If only I could keep things that way.

Chapter Eleven

Small-town hardware stores were supposed to be a bastion of the local community—a place where people could come together for the sharing of knowledge, ideas, and overall camaraderie as residents explored their DIY capabilities. What they were not supposed to be were battlegrounds. Reverie Springs Hardware had somehow skittered off the bastion track and into the battle area.

I rushed out the back receiving door with Elmer on my heels, following the sounds of yelling and arguing that had seeped through the walls and windows. The scene I came upon was one I never would have expected. Aunt Gwendolyn stood behind an obviously agitated Ander, both seemingly facing off against Joan, Miss Rose's sister and leash-law missionary.

"What is going on back here?"

None of them looked happy. They also didn't answer me.

I had to try again, choosing the calmest of the three to focus on. "Ander, what—"

"I think it's time for you to go, Joan," he said, still not looking at me.

Joan didn't move an inch, though there was definite wobbling happening with her. "You don't get to tell me what to do, Ander Mendoza."

"And you don't get to come here and attack Miss Gwen that way," he said, still keeping himself between Joan and Aunt Gwendolyn. He was wearing his chef's coat, which likely meant he'd been inside the diner cooking before whatever was going on had kicked off outside. Once again, coming to our rescue. The man was basically a knight in shining armor...without the armor.

But if he had felt the need to protect my aunt, I deserved to know from what. "Is someone going to tell me what's going on?"

"Oh, now you want communication?" Joan slurred the last syllable of that word, tottering as she spun in my direction. "Funny how you want what you don't give."

I...had no clue what she meant. "I'm not sure what I was supposed to be communicating to you, Joan. But maybe—"

"Shut up, Brylie," she spat, that hard glare spearing me in place. "You know exactly what you've done."

I thought hard—I really did—but I came up with nothing. "Nope. I don't."

That denial seemed to enrage Joan, who quite literally growled at me. "Quit lying to me. You and your aunt, always trying to appear so kind and generous when, deep down, you're both taking advantage of those around you."

Aunt Gwendolyn hissed out a quiet, "Joan, stop—"

"How dare you reopen the store without telling me?" Joan screamed, interrupting my aunt. "This was my sister's place."

Elmer growled, but I shushed him. No sense attracting more of her ire. "I don't understand. We're not open yet."

"But you will be," she said, still glaring my way. She wasn't wrong. Eventually, I would reopen the store. Once it—and I—were ready. Which was not today.

Of course, she didn't need to know that, so I leaned against the back wall and crossed my arms over my chest, faking much more attitude than I actually felt in that moment. "Okay, so let's lay this out. The store was Rose's, and I'm really sorry for your loss. But this is my store now, and I get to decide what to do with it."

"It shouldn't be your store. She was *my* sister. You should have at least asked me if reopening was the right thing to do."

It was Aunt Gwendolyn who responded to that one. "We've gone over this, Joan. The lawyers have gone over this with you. The store was left to me, so I get to choose what happens to it, and I choose to let Brylie take the helm."

"It's wrong, and what's even worse is you didn't have the guts to tell me yourself, Gwen. You let me find out through others that my sister's place had been taken over." She took a step closer to Aunt Gwendolyn, her eyes red and her face twisted into a pained sort of scowl. One that turned to pure rage when Elmer barked at her. "That dog needs a leash."

Her obsession with leashes knew no end.

"He doesn't," I said. "He never has."

"I'll call the sheriff on you. I'll call animal control. I'll kill the da—"

"You will do no such thing." Aunt Gwendolyn looked ready to spit nails as she pointed a finger at Joan. "You should try minding your own business, Joan."

"And *you* should have told me what was happening with Rose's store instead of letting me find out from Corbin Lamb. It's wrong." Joan turned as if to leave, shaking her head with every step. "You've always been wrong, Gwendolyn."

My aunt visibly deflated, her face falling and showing her

age for once. Those words from Joan seemed harsher than I would have expected to hear regarding something as basic as the reopening of a closed business, but the woman wasn't sticking around to explain herself and I certainly wasn't chasing her down. Instead, I waited until she disappeared around the corner, kneeling by Elmer to make sure he didn't do anything stupid like run after her. Or walk after, more likely. Elmer didn't exactly have attack hound on his pedigree.

When Ander—who'd been silently holding back, or up, Aunt Gwendolyn—finally relaxed, I rose to my feet, pushing off the wall and taking the few steps toward my aunt. The old woman needed a moment, but she also had some explaining to do.

"What the heck was that?"

Aunt Gwendolyn straightened herself, still appearing far more shaken than I would have expected. At least for a moment. A deep breath and a braid pat later, she raised her chin and wore her haughtiest look. "Joan has always been a little salty when it comes to Rose's will, is all."

The slang...I couldn't get past it. "Salty?"

Ander coughed a sort of snort-laugh. "She likes to keep current."

"Hush, you two," Aunt Gwendolyn said, her voice a little more normal. Coming back to herself with every passing second. "I'm allowed to expand my vocabulary."

And I was allowed to question her...on everything. "So, what happened? What was Joan doing back here?"

"I don't really know," Aunt Gwendolyn said. "I had been coming down to invite you to lunch when Joan showed up at the back door."

Which explained part of the situation. I still didn't know why Ander had been out there. "And you?"

"I was taking out the trash and ran into the two of them arguing," Ander said. "I never have liked the way Joan talks to Miss Gwen, so I stuck around to make sure things stayed civil." He shrugged. "They didn't."

Of course not. "Thank you for stepping in."

He nodded, keeping his eyes on me. Pausing for a long moment before finally asking what he apparently wanted to. "Nothing bad happening at the house? Still sleeping okay?"

Same questions he'd been asking me every day since he had woken up on my couch. Since he had offered to sleep over whenever I wanted him to...and since I'd been refusing him. "Nothing bad happening and sleeping okay."

Okay being the operative word—I hadn't returned to sleep in the house since that night. I couldn't bring myself to. Sleeping on a minivan seat was getting way old but was the preferable option to being alone in that rambling, creaky house.

"I think it's time for me to head inside," Aunt Gwendolyn said, turning for the entrance, her soft gray cardigan fluttering a bit with the movement. "Come, Brylie. I've made a pot of chili and some fresh bread. I'd like it if you joined me for lunch."

Not a question—more of a demand. One I wasn't going to fight. "Sure. C'mon, Elmer."

Ander grabbed my arm, stopping me with a gentle tug. "I'll take him. I noticed he didn't eat as much as usual at breakfast, so I made him some chicken and rice in case he has an upset stomach."

The chef cooking for my dog should have been unusual, but it wasn't. Ander always had something set aside for Elmer. My poor Basset hound would never win any swimwear competitions, but his girth made it obvious that he was well cared for in every chubby inch. "Are you sure you don't mind?"

"It's no trouble. Just come by and grab him later."

I turned to unlock the door, all three of us walking into the receiving area of the store with Elmer padding alongside Ander as if he knew where he was going next. Aunt Gwendolyn and I headed to the back stairs leading to her apartment while Ander waited, watching us leave.

"Does the door lock on its own?" he asked.

I nodded, sending him a smile. "It does. Thanks."

"Any time. You two lock that door as well once inside and have a good lunch. Come with me, Elmer boy."

The two males walked back outside, Ander closing the door behind him. Aunt Gwendolyn led me up the stairs and directly to her little dining table—after locking the door, of course—quickly serving up two bowls of chili with slices of crusty bread. But even though the food smelled amazing—and it really did—I couldn't concentrate on my meal.

After just two small bites, I put my spoon down. "I need to know what's going on with Joan."

Aunt Gwendolyn didn't even look up. "What do you mean?"

"*I mean* she showed up here and harassed you. I'd like to know why."

"She's just hurt that I didn't tell her the store would be reopening."

No itch, but something still didn't sit right with me. "Why does it matter whether you tell her or not?"

She finally looked right at me, bathing me in that sadness she carried. That sense of loss and loneliness. And a little bit of guilt as well.

"Because she loved Rosie. Those two had a volatile relationship, but they cared for each other. Rosie's death hit Joan awfully hard. The will, Rose leaving me the store, it was a bit of a surprise to Joan." She shrugged and refocused on her food, stirring the chili slowly. "Not that it should have been."

Comments like that last one always made me feel as if I'd somehow forgotten something important. As if I were missing pieces of the puzzle. And I was, though not because my memory had failed me. Because I'd never been told the full story in the first place. There was still so much I didn't know about Gwendolyn and Rose and Joan...about Reverie Springs in general, really. It was about time I got some answers.

Time to tear off the bandage, so to speak. "What happened to Rose?"

Aunt Gwendolyn sat still and silent for a long moment, not answering. Not breathing, it seemed. But then she sighed.

"Car accident," she said, her lips tight and her words clipped. "She'd been on her way home from the store when she drove right off the road and flipped the car. The sheriff found a dog lying dead on the side of the asphalt. He figured it must have run out in front of her and Rose overcorrected."

No wonder the entire town seemed obsessed with leashes. "So she died suddenly."

Aunt Gwendolyn nodded. "Yes."

Poor Rose. Such a horrible way to die—an unplanned accident leaving you no time to say goodbye. It was heartbreaking, really. And totally relatable considering what I'd been through with my dad.

I scratched at a subtle itch along my wrist before grabbing Aunt Gwendolyn's hand across the table. "I'm truly sorry for your loss."

"I know you are, just as I'm sorry for yours." She squeezed my fingers. "Your father died awfully quick as well."

He had—one minute, he'd been fine, and the next, not so

much. Massive heart attacks tended to do that, much like car accidents.

Thinking about my dad wasn't going to help anything, though. "All loss is hard."

"Indeed." Aunt Gwen smiled and patted my hand one last time before sitting back and letting me go. Watching me with those green eyes that always seemed to see more than most. "On to happier subjects. When do you think you'll get the store opened?"

That question had my stomach turning to lead, and I shook my head as I stared into my bowl. "A few more weeks, maybe. I'd like to get a little work done on the house before I lock myself into the retail schedule."

Aunt Gwendolyn sat quiet for a few seconds, the tension growing between us. I thought for sure she'd hold out until I said more, but she eventually huffed in what sounded an awful lot like defeat.

"Whenever you're ready, dear. Speaking of the manor, I'd like to help you revamp the window boxes. The front of the house is looking so beautiful, but the landscaping has fallen out of repair."

I darted a look up at her. "Really? You don't have to. I would never ask you to put in that much work."

Even though I would totally love it if someone—anyone— would take that task off my hands.

Aunt Gwendolyn seemed ready to do just that. "Work, schmork. I used to love planting at the manor. Rose and I planted huge gardens and so many different herbs and flowers for my spells. It would be a pleasure to get my hands back in the dirt there."

Point made. "If you'd like to do some gardening around the house, I'd be happy for the help."

"Good. And you just tell me if I end up being a nuisance."

"You'd never be a nuisance. You're welcome to come dig in the dirt any time you'd like."

"Thank you," she said, grinning my way. "That would be a nice reminder of better times. Plus, then I could teach you some of the art of being a witch. Help you learn to control that power of yours."

The power I was not supposed to talk about, according to my dad. "I think I'm doing just fine."

"Oh, dear child. If this is fine, you have a long way to go. Hiding your power isn't fine—it's counterintuitive. Nature wants you to feel her."

"It's not nature I'm worried about—it's all the people who seem to have emotions strong enough to overtake my own."

Aunt Gwendolyn grabbed for my hand again, holding my gaze. This time, I didn't feel so overwhelmed by her pain, didn't want to crawl under a rock and cry looking into the soft green eyes. No, this time, she held all that pain and hurt back. I didn't know how, but she did.

"You can learn," she said, her voice quiet but strong as she seemed to answer my unspoken question. "The way to keep your own emotions from being tainted by others—you can learn it. That sort of avoidance is a practicable skill."

One I probably shouldn't have even been thinking about. "My dad always said—"

"Your dad didn't like the fact that your mother came from a long line of powerful female witches. He took your mother from us to distance her from her gifts—something she agreed to," she said, hands up as if expecting me to attack her for speaking poorly about my dad. "But you...you came home. It's time to reclaim your place as a Laveau witch, Brylie. The town needs you."

I doubted that, but I didn't dismiss her. And I certainly wasn't about to turn down her offer.

"Fine. You come plant and teach me. I'll be your willing student."

At least for a while.

Chapter Twelve

Mike Allen walked into the hardware store the next day, looking slightly irritated and very sweaty. Not surprising, considering the number of boxes he'd been carrying inside for me.

"This is the last one." He set the crate down beside the others and grabbed his tablet from the hook on his belt, scanning the barcode to acknowledge the delivery of the product. "I just need your signature here, and you'll be all set."

I opened the crate first, taking a quick peek at all the products as I'd been doing with every one he'd brought to me. Picking orders in a warehouse wasn't a foolproof job, and I liked to at least make sure everything looked as expected before I signed off on the delivery. Not that I could know for sure without doing a full inventory; I had ordered a lot of stuff to replace the stock in the store. Too much to memorize, but that was okay. I had all day to check the products in.

"Thanks, Mike. I appreciate your help bringing everything in."

"It's no problem. It'll actually be nice to see this old place open again. It always was a good store, and Miss Rose really helped the community when they needed it."

Between the stories of Rose and memories of my dad's store, I knew I had some big shoes to fill in running this store. I felt the pressure on a daily basis, but I had most of the selling space set up, and I had scrubbed the store almost spotless. I'd been taught from a young age how to take care of the customers who would eventually walk through the door and how to run a small business like this one. I could do this.

I may have wanted to puke every day as I grappled with setting an actual grand reopening date, but I could handle it.

Maybe.

Mike had been gone for a couple of hours when someone knocked on the front doors to the store. That was new—in the few weeks I'd been working in the space, not one person had come to those doors. The ones I would soon be unlocking and opening for all the townspeople to walk through so they could shop.

My gut twisted just as I expected it to. Pressure was cruel.

I'd papered over the front doors so no one passing by could see the mess the store had been during my clean-up phase, which meant I couldn't tell who waited outside until I swung open the door. I regretted that fact immediately.

"Brylie. You're looking lovely today."

Corbin Lamb stood on the sidewalk outside the door, smiling at me in that snake-oil–salesman way that never did look quite right. He also had a business card in his hand and a strong hopeful vibe filling the air around him.

Sales-pitch time.

"Mr. Lamb. Is there something I can help you with today?" I leaned against the doorframe, blocking his entrance. Making it clear he wasn't getting inside.

He definitely noticed. "I was hoping you'd be up for a little conversation about your business plans. I was a big customer of Miss Rose's—I'd love the see the new setup."

I might as well have rolled around naked in a pile of poison ivy for how itchy my entire body became with that particular lie. Whatever he wanted, it had nothing to do with my new floor plan. "Now's not a good time. I have a shipment to inventory and stock to put up."

"It would only be for a few minutes. I have a lot of ideas on how I can help make this store a success once more."

"Honestly, Mr. Lamb—"

"Please," he said, grinning even wider and showing off that ultra-white smile. "Call me Corbin."

"Fine. Corbin, I really don't have time to discuss the success of this store because I need to get it ready to open. Perhaps if you called first or set up an appointment." Which would never happen because I wouldn't answer his call, nor would I attend any sort of meeting with him, but he didn't need to know that just yet.

Avoidance—I lived it.

"Of course. I can understand you're likely overwhelmed, but I just feel it's my duty to make sure you know that Main Street properties are nearly worthless right now." He shook his head, appearing almost heartbroken at the very idea of having to say such a thing. But then his smile returned. "Now, the manor—that's got some serious potential. There's a lot of money tied up in those fields, money that could help you grow your new business. Give you a leg up on that success you'll be chasing."

I stared at him, not speaking. Not wanting to have this conversation. I still wasn't convinced he wasn't the one breaking in to the manor. I certainly wasn't going to give him an all-access pass that being the Realtor selling the place would provide. Did he think I was stupid?

The answer to that was likely yes.

Eventually, the awkward silence I refused to break got to him. His smile fell, his overall demeanor becoming decidedly less bright and predator-like. Instead, he looked like a man who'd just failed to close a deal. Which he was.

"Well, I can see you're busy. I'll leave you to it." He moved as if to turn away before bringing his arm up, snapping his fingers, and chuckling a bit. "Oh, and by the way, I set up the contract with Thomas Lee regarding the farm field rental, which ends after this season. If you want to extend that contract, I'd be happy to help you renegotiate."

Of course he had set up that deal—renting anything in this town likely went through him. Just what I needed.

"I've discussed this with Thomas already and I think we can come to our own agreement, but thank you for the reminder."

"Of course," he said, gnashing his teeth and twisting his lips as if he'd just bit into a lemon. "Again, if there's anything you need—"

"I know where to find you. Have a great day." I slipped back inside, shutting and locking the door behind me. Elmer came out from around the cash wrap, looking decidedly irritable. He didn't seem to like being left out of my chat.

"You weren't exactly much help there, mister."

"Are you talking to me or the dog?" Ander strolled around the corner, both scaring me and giving me a thrill. I liked him being in my store, liked the way he took up so much space in the aisle with his wide shoulders and his beard and his air of grumpiness. What I didn't like was someone coming inside when they shouldn't have been able to.

"Where'd you come from?" I asked, trying hard not to let the panic consume me.

"I came in through the back."

"You have a key?" Not possible, considering I'd changed the locks after I'd figured out Mike had had a key, but that really had been my first thought. Not the smartest assumption, but oh well.

Ander didn't point out my folly. "No. The door was unlocked."

That wasn't likely. "It should lock automatically when it closes behind someone. It should have closed behind Mike after he finished today's delivery."

Ander frowned. "You think someone tampered with it?"

I didn't even let him finish the question before I took off at a fast walk, hurrying down the aisles to the storeroom and then to the large door we used for receiving. Did I think someone had tampered with it? Yes. It was the only thing that made any sort of sense as to how the door hadn't been latched.

What was with me and doors lately?

When I reached the entrance, I gave the slab of metal a shove, making sure not to touch the handle. The door swung open without my having to unlatch it in any way.

"It's definitely broken." I squatted down, inspecting the door itself before moving on to the jamb. "You have to be kidding me."

Ander leaned over my shoulder. "What?"

I grabbed a pen from my pocket and poked it into the latch strike, angling and tugging until I pulled out the pen with a wad of sticky pink stuff on the end.

I held it up so Ander could see. "Gum."

The chef backed up. "It's been chewed."

"Well...yeah. That way, it's malleable enough to stick in there."

"That's disgusting." He retreated some more, looking as if he might be the one to puke soon. "You should get rid of all that."

The reaction felt strong. Too strong. "Ander, do you not like gum?"

He looked from me to the pen and back. "I don't like gum that's been in someone's mouth. That's just foul."

Point made. Not wanting to upset him more, I stood up, tossing the pen and gum into the trash before closing the door. This time, the lock worked. "They blocked the latch bolt from engaging, making my lock useless. What a ridiculous thing to do."

"You sure you haven't had any more problems out at the house?"

"Not that I know of."

Which obviously wasn't what he had wanted to hear. "I'm not sure I like that answer."

Yeah, me neither. "Elmer would let me know if he sensed someone around the house. He's been quiet, so I assume we've been alone."

Ander huffed what sounded way too much like a grunt, as if the very idea of relying on my dog somehow offended him. "If you need me to come out or a new place to stay—"

"I'm fine." I put my hand up, stopping the argument I knew he likely wanted to start. No way was I burdening him with me and my dog, though. That simply would not happen. I could stand on my own two feet—even if standing meant hunching over in my minivan as I tried to climb into the seat I used for a bed. "Really. Elmer and I are doing okay out there."

"Fine. But the offer stands," Ander said, whistling for

Elmer in a surprisingly successful way. "It's dinnertime, and I want to feed you two. Come to the diner with me for an early meal."

That sounded like the best plan of the day. "Fine. Let me just make sure the front is locked up."

"I'll take Elmer with me. Meet us in the diner."

"Sounds good." I hurried through the store, flipping off all the lights and locking the front entrance. Checking it three separate times just in case. I needed that door well and truly locked.

On my way back into the storeroom, I popped into the office to grab my tablet then headed for the door. The one that had been messed with. The one someone had intentionally sabotaged so they could access my store. What could they be hoping to gain from that? There wasn't much street value in the place—no computers or even bigger power tools, nothing easily sold via social media garage sale listings. It really made no sense.

I also wasn't sure who would have done such a thing. The obvious choice was Mike—he'd been inside the store, and he'd had access to the door without my being present. But would he have done that? I'd never noticed him chewing gum, and he'd likely left the door open to bring the boxes in and out. Someone walking by could have shoved the gum in the lock as a joke or to set up a later robbery. I just didn't know, and I doubted I was going to find out any time soon.

Once I had the store locked up tight, I hurried through the alley and into the back door of the restaurant. Ander had given me permission to come and go that way, especially with Elmer, as it was a little quicker than running around front. The only bad part about it was that I had no idea who was actually in the restaurant until I came through the hallway and past the restrooms. Normally, not a big deal. Apparently, this was not a normally sort of night.

"I just want to know where she is so I can talk to her!" A loud and quite obviously drunk Joan Turlington stood in the middle of the dining area, yelling at Ander. "Why are you hiding her from me?"

There was no way to hide or escape—I'd already appeared, and it took only a second for Joan to spot me.

"You," she said, hurrying my way. "I want to talk to your aunt. Where is she?"

This was one I could answer honestly. "I have no idea. I haven't seen her all day."

"How is that possible? I just want to talk to the old hag. Why are you people lying to me?"

I glanced at Ander, who had already angled himself to easily slip between Joan and me. He did not look happy.

"You've had too much to drink, Joan." He reached for her arm. "How about you take a seat, and I'll bring you some dinner."

Joan snatched her arm away from him. "I don't want your food, Ander. I just want to know where Gwen is."

"I can't tell you that."

"Fine," she spat, glaring down at Elmer, who'd situated himself at my side. "And you'd better hope I don't call the health department on you. Dogs do not belong in restaurants."

With that, she spun on her heel and hurried out the door, leaving Ander and me alone in his empty restaurant. His mood had definitely soured, his anger a palpable energy slowly filling the space around us. Me? I had lost my appetite.

"I hate to bail on you, but I suddenly feel like I should just go home."

Ander's dark eyes locked on mine for a fleeting moment

before taking a trip around my face as if looking for something to tell him what was going on in my head. "You okay?"

Not really. Joan's behavior had thrown me, but sometimes a little fibbing was worth the itch. "Yeah, I just...want to go home."

Home. To Willow Manor. And the shelter of my minivan.

"Sure. Of course. Let me just get you and Elmer a carryout package."

"You don't have—"

"I know I don't have to, but if I don't send you home with something, I'll worry all night that you haven't eaten. So, please...allow me this."

Grumpy beast and a big softy, what a combination. At my nod of acceptance—because really, I *would* eventually be hungry—Ander hurried off while I took a seat at a table in the back with my trusty Basset hound at my feet. The day had been too long—first Mike, then Corbin, then Joan. All people I thought might be the ones breaking in to the manor. All wanting something that had been given to me. The very thought of it all exhausted me.

Thirty minutes, two large bags of food, and a promise to Ander to call or text if I was at all even nervous at the house, I pulled up to the manor. Everything seemed the way it had been when I'd left, but I still felt a bit of unease. I brushed it off, unlocking the front door and holding it open for Elmer to come inside. I nearly kicked myself, though, when I walked into the kitchen and spotted someone in the shadows of the garden. Thomas stood with his back to the house, looking over the bushes planted on the far side of the deck. Way too close to be checking on his fields.

Without thinking about how things could go wrong— because they really, really could have—I slipped out the conservatory door and worked my way toward the corner of the house. Hoping to catch Thomas in the act and figure out what he'd been doing.

A man appeared in my way before I could get there, though. One who wasn't the local farmer renting my fields.

"Oh," I said, stumbling back a step. "Carl. You scared me. What are you doing here?"

"Just coming to check on you." The old man didn't look thrilled to see me, though. "What are you doing all the way over there, girl? Were you trying to play hide-and-seek?"

As if I had the time...or anyone to play with. "No. I saw someone through the window and thought I'd check on them."

"That was just old Thomas Lee. He's out checking the blueberry bushes."

"He grows blueberries in my landscaping?" Because he definitely hadn't been out in the fields.

Did blueberries even grow in fields? I had no idea.

"Nah," Carl said, waving me off. "Rose planted them. But Thomas takes care of the bushes since she's passed on. He's good about sharing the crop from her old plants now that no one else is here to enjoy them."

"That seems...nice."

"Yeah. Not sure why Miss Gwen doesn't come out to get a share. They were some of her favorites. Rose actually planted them for her."

That sounded so sweet. "Aunt Gwen used to let Rose plant whatever she wanted, huh?"

His brow furrowed in what looked like confusion, and he cocked his head a little. "Well, I mean, it was her garden."

"Who her?"

"Miss Rose. This manor was her house too. Didn't you know?"

That would be a *no*, and there was not an itch in sight, so he was definitely telling the truth. Aunt Gwen had shared the house with her business partner.

Why hadn't she told me?

Chapter Thirteen

S leep had begun to elude me the longer I put off the store's grand opening. It wasn't as if I wasn't tired; it was simply that my mind refused to slow down and rest. Would the customers come back to the store? Would I be friendly enough to attract people to a business in such an isolated community? Would I ever be able to walk into a hardware store without thinking of my dad? Would I ever get a chance to actually live inside the house instead of in my minivan?

If I'd had a Magic 8-Ball to shake, my guess would be I'd be getting a lot of "reply hazy, try again" and "concentrate and ask again" responses.

"I do not understand what's happening here." I turned to look over my shoulder and sighed. No sense talking to Elmer—he was passed out across the foyer against the stairs. It was just me and what I had to assume was a leaky sink. I'd come home to a little bit of water on the repaired wood floors. Again. I was so darn tired of water. "Fine. I'll just keep...replacing things. Without help. No problem, Elmer."

I would have sworn his snoring actually rose in volume.

Not that there was anything I could do about it. It wasn't Elmer's fault I was suffering through a bout of insomnia. Besides, I had plenty to do to keep me busy. Like replacing the water supply lines to the pedestal sink in the powder room. For the third time.

I gripped my wrench tight, loosening the cold-water line with little more than a good, strong tug. A bit of water poured out onto the towel I had laid under the lines, but nothing too bad. I'd turned off the supply and drained the lines as much as possible. The last thing I needed was more water damage. It only took me a few minutes to remove the line from the faucet and replace it, adding a couple rounds of plumber's tape at each joint for added protection. I would banish the leaks if it was the last thing I did.

"Got it," I said to an empty house and a sleeping dog, wiping off my hands and grabbing the damp towels from under the lines. "There is no reason for this sink to be leaking. None at all."

Didn't mean I wouldn't come home to find water in the foyer again, though.

I yawned as I packed up my tools, the late hour and my lack of sleep suddenly catching up with me. One more thing—I just wanted to accomplish one more thing. That door to the third floor still hadn't opened for me, but I'd brought home a few tools to pick the lock. This was my house now; I should have access to every inch of it.

So, I headed up the stairs—stepping over Elmer, who didn't move a muscle—and walked straight to the skinny door. With far more hesitation than I would ever admit to, I reached for the handle. Locked. Still. The hows and whys of that single door being locked in an empty house definitely tried to battle to the forefront of my mind, but I refused to contemplate them. That would make me put off picking the lock, which was my second goal of the night. Fix the sink, pick the lock. I'd been chanting it all day.

One more thing.

Tool pouch in hand, I set out to fix the last problem of the night. It took longer than I'd expected. Much longer. Long enough that Elmer actually woke up, climbed the stairs, and came to join me in the second-floor hall. I hadn't even realized it until he plopped right behind me, nearly knocking me into the door. His snores were a calming accompaniment to my picking of the lock.

"It makes *no* sense." I tossed the flashlight I'd been using to the floor, sitting back on my heels and looking over the door again. The still-locked door. "No hinges to pop, no keyway to pick, no way to access the latch bolt, and no mounting bolts to take apart. It's like...the door isn't locked. It just doesn't want to open."

I reached for my phone and immediately moaned my frustration. It wasn't in my pocket. I must have left it in the powder room downstairs.

"Wonderful. I can't fix the door, and I can't google what the heck could be wrong with it to figure out why. This is not my night."

Elmer sighed and groaned, making his disinterest known. But as I sat there looking over the door and letting the puzzle of why the lock that wasn't technically locked wouldn't release, the groaning of my Basset hound turned to more of a growl. And it grew louder.

When Elmer rose to his feet and hurried toward the top of the stairs, I knew we were in trouble.

"Hang on, boy." I grabbed the biggest tool at my disposal —the wrench I'd been using on the sink in the powder room—

and slipped quietly and carefully to the stairs. "Let's keep the growling to a minimum, okay? Don't want to give our position away."

Elmer huffed but then quieted, following silently behind me as I snuck down the stairs. We kept to the very side of the treads to keep the squeaks and groans of the wood to a minimum, both of us moving slowly, deliberately. And...in a posture that got my brain spinning.

Why is it that when sneaking, people sort of...duck? As if being six inches shorter than normal makes one invisible. That was my thought as I made it to the landing and followed the stairs to the main floor. While ducking. The entire act made no sense.

I did it anyway.

Thankfully, the foyer stood empty, so Elmer and I made it to that level without being seen. The only open room directly off the foyer was the study, which sat similarly empty. That led to the issue of how to investigate the other rooms. The house was set up with one long hallway bisecting the space. An entrance opened to the study on one side, but there was no such entryway on the other like you might expect. You had to walk down the hall and through the family room to access the front room on that side of the house. The kitchen and dining room were behind the study along the hall, the glass-wall conservatory past the kitchen. There was no way to examine all the rooms without either being seen...or trapped.

I was shaking by the time I made it to the hallway, fully trembling as I peeked around the corner. Nothing seemed out of sorts except the French doors at the end leading to the deck that sat ajar. They had definitely not only been closed but locked earlier.

Someone had broken into the house. Again.

"Okay, Elmer," I whispered, clutching my wrench and really wishing I had my phone on me. Feeling stupid for not grabbing it as I passed the powder room. "We're going to need a diversion. Something to scare them, if possible."

He stared up at me with his big brown eyes, those ears hanging almost to the floor. Looking so very regal in that moment. I didn't need regal—I needed wild.

"Elmer," I said, louder than a whisper, for sure. Making certain I had his attention. My dog may have been lazy, but he knew a few commands. Including one that was about to come in handy. "Speak."

The dog barked loudly, turning the sharp bursts of sounds into long, rolling howls as we ran down the hall and toward the entrances to the kitchen and family room. I thought I was going to have to choose a direction to go in as I couldn't be in both places, but that decision was made for me when a person in all black with a ski mask over their face ran out of the family room and through the French doors. They disappeared into the night, leaving me shaken and breathless.

And tired of listening to Elmer howl.

"Good boy," I said, patting his head and letting him know he could stop. "Let's just...yeah."

I locked the doors, taking a long moment to calm myself, before moving to inspect where that person had come from. I crept through the family room and tried to take in every detail. Nothing looked disturbed, nothing sat out of place. The weird little room beyond it also appeared completely normal—seemingly exactly as it had been left. And how it had been left was a big mess.

The room made no sense design-wise or in the flow of the house. You had to walk through the family room and then pass through what looked like a closet-turned-hallway to access the space. Once inside, a single shelf about waist-high was nestled in the niche between the closet-hall and an actual closet to the left. A big bay window allowed in a lot of light from the front of the house, and it connected to an angled wall which seemed to work its way around the corner of the porch to join the entry. Odd for sure.

The space was a nice size—perhaps meant to be a parlor or living room. Whatever it had been intended for didn't matter because it had become a junk room. Random stuff sat everywhere. Boxes and shelves lined with trinkets, papers, and books. The floor almost completely covered in stacks of furniture and more boxes. All things I simply hadn't had time to deal with yet. Could this have been what the intruder had been looking for? Something in this room? The family room only contained a few pieces of furniture—there wasn't really anything in there to want to take.

But what could be in the mess of the strange room that someone would want to steal?

And how on earth were they ballsy enough to walk into the house when I was obviously inside?

I needed to figure out who kept breaking into my house and fast, because next time, if there was a next time, they might not want to run from me.

Chapter Fourteen

The next morning—after once again sleeping inside my locked minivan—my need to figure out who kept breaking in to my house felt just as strong as it had the night before. And seemed just as crazy. I had a list of possible suspects in my phone, a sense of urgency from the fact that the intruder kept getting so close to me, and no real plan other than to find the people on the list and talk to them. That was it. Have a conversation with someone who could be a thief.

See? Crazy.

"Come on, Elmer." I held the van door open for him, finally leaning down to help him into the passenger seat when he huffed for the third time. The dog seemed tired and cranky, which I related to for sure. "Once we figure out who keeps breaking in, we'll get them to stop bothering us, then we can move in to the house. Okay?"

Elmer didn't answer. He barely even looked at me as I fastened his doggie seat belt. In fact, he totally ignored me.

This was going to be a long day.

We drove into town with the radio playing softly in the

background, passing trees and farm fields along the way. Reverie Springs didn't have much, but what it had was obviously cared for. No abandoned homes or derelict structures. Everything appeared tidy and relatively up-to-date; even the empty storefronts along Main Street didn't look abandoned or neglected. Every single building and window seemed to practically sparkle in the sun.

It was a little creepy, to be honest. A little too fake. Like the people were trying just a little bit too hard.

Instead of stopping at the hardware store, I headed straight to the local office of one Corbin Lamb—real estate agent and master of smarm. I was almost hoping he'd call me Rylie again today and then refuse to apologize for it like the first time we met. I really liked the idea of calling him Colton just to piss him off again.

Sadly for me, the man seemed to have learned my real name.

"Brylie." He stood from his desk as soon as I walked in, grinning my way and offering me his hand long before he had reached me. His energy filled me, the feeling of opportunity and possibilities high. My sudden appearance at this place of work had made the man near giddy. "How are you today? Do you want some coffee or a water?"

I did, but not from him. I had a feeling taking anything would be seen as part of a negotiation. Like I'd somehow owe him for that bottle of water. "No, thank you. I just popped in to chat with you about the manor. If you have time, of course."

His eyes lit up in a way that told me he'd find the time if he didn't have it, and the air sizzled around him. Giddy had become an understatement. "I always have time for you, dear. Come. Sit down."

I did as he requested, settling into the chair on the other

side of his desk. Elmer didn't plop as usual, though. Instead, he sat right beside me with his head up and his eyes firmly locked on the man across the desk from me. Something Corbin definitely noticed and wasn't fond of, if the look of disgust that flashed across his face was any indication. The man didn't like my dog, but, more importantly, my dog didn't like him.

Corbin sat straight, attentive and focused. Business mode activated, apparently. "So...the manor. How can I help you with it?"

Time to lie. "I've been thinking about what you said the other day, about the house being a windfall for me because of the land. I'd like to get a few specifics, if I could."

"Of course." He reached into a drawer and pulled out a folder. The tab said Willow Manor, and inside was a lot more paperwork than I would have ever expected for someone who didn't own or have a stake in the property. Guess he *really* wanted to sell the manor...and had for a long time. "The manor sits on 120 acres of land comprised primarily of woods and farm fields. That's a lot of land."

It was. It really was. What had Aunt Gwendolyn been thinking, giving me so much...stuff? "And what sort of market is there for land all the way out here in Reverie Springs?"

"You wouldn't think too much, but they just opened a new distribution center for Aldazon Shipping over in Hilton. Lots of new jobs for the area, and people want the quiet, small-town feel they get in Reverie Springs. I'd recommend dividing the land and selling off a few parts for subdivision expansion." When I didn't speak, he leaned forward over the desktop. "Tract homes, you know? Detached condo-style."

Yes, I knew, but he liked being the smartest man in the room, and I liked letting him think he was...for the moment.

"Right," I said, pursing my lips as if thinking hard. "Not all the land, though."

"Oh, goodness no," he replied with a laugh. "We'd keep fifteen acres with the house so you can sell that behemoth as a country estate. No one wants neighbors right up on them."

Except the people in those tract houses he had visions of building. "And you tried to convince my aunt Gwendolyn to do this?"

"I did. I thought she needed a little less responsibility than the manor required, but she refused to even consider it. She wanted the manor and the grounds to remain whole." He scoffed. "Don't know why—she never did anything with all that land."

"Except lease it out."

Corbin shook his head. "What Thomas rents from the manor is nothing compared to the possibility of income that you'd get from selling. It's pennies, when the manor land should be worth—" his lips pulled up and spread as he threw me a villainous smile, his face transforming like some sort of cartoon wolf "—well, a heck of a lot more than pennies."

Elmer huffed beside me, letting his displeasure at his being forced to stay awake to protect me be known. The time to wrap this up had come, but there were still a few things I needed to know.

"You negotiated the land deal with Thomas Lee...the leasing of the farm fields. Yes?"

Corbin sat back. "I did, even renegotiated with him after Rose died so Miss Gwen could continue to earn money off what little of the property he used. The taxes on the place would have bankrupted her, I reckon."

I doubted that, but I wasn't about to get into a fight right then. "So, you knew Rose, then."

He laughed, a sarcastic lilt to it, if a laugh could be sarcastic.

"Everyone in Reverie Springs knew Rose. You won't find a person who didn't have some sort of interaction with her, and we all loved her. That car accident was a right tragedy."

I nodded, contemplating. He seemed sincere enough, but was he? Would he steal from her home, her memory, just to make a buck even though he *loved* her? Maybe.

But as Corbin reached to grab his coffee mug, I got a good look at his hands. Clean hands. Soft ones, by the look of them. I'd grown up in a hardware store and had seen hundreds of thousands of hands. The ones of men and women who truly worked on their homes, the ones of people who were more the buy-it-yourself type than the do-it-yourself. I'd seen lots of hands, and they all told a story about the person they were attached to. Corbin's hands were no different—the man wasn't into physical labor. At all. Those hands were smooth and clean with no scratches or scars, no calluses or swollen knuckles. The thief had pulled out a full mantel and carried that hunk of wood out the door. Corbin didn't seem like the type who would—one—be able to do that—and, two—be willing to put in the work. He seemed more...manipulative. Opportunistic, sure, but not when physicality was involved.

Or maybe I wasn't giving him enough credit.

And I really needed to stop staring at his hands before he got the wrong idea.

"The house has sustained some damage," I said, going in for my last bit of research. "It would need some repairs done to be ready for the market. When I sold my dad's house—" I clenched my hands, my wrists itching like crazy as I twisted the truth of that particular situation to fit this one "—the real estate agent came to help with some of that. Is that a service you provide?"

Corbin laughed again. "Oh no, I don't fix things. I hire people, though. Let me get you a list of local handymen who might be able to help you out."

He rose to his feet, leaving me to wallow in my feeling of failure. Corbin was not the thief. I mean, he could have been, but my doubts were way high. The man hadn't lied to me the whole time I'd been talking with him, and it certainly didn't seem like yanking that mantel had been high on his list of things to do. No, Corbin wasn't handy enough to be the thief. My instincts on that detail felt strong and sure. Which meant it was time to go find my next suspect.

"Here." Corbin handed me a piece of paper from the printer with names and numbers on it. "Any one of these people would likely be willing to help for the right price. I can vouch for all of them, too."

There were a few names on the list I already knew—Mike Allen, the delivery driver for the hardware store and someone I thought might be stealing from the manor, and Carl Reese, old man and neighbor to the manor. The rest meant nothing, but I figured I'd run the list past Aunt Gwendolyn, see if any of them gave us new options for people who might be stealing from us. And scaring the heck out of me.

"Thank you," I said, rising to my feet. Elmer followed my lead, huffing but keeping close to my ankles. Not letting Corbin out of his sight for a second. "If I decide to move forward on anything, I'll let you know."

"Of course." Corbin led me to the door, glaring down at Elmer almost the entire way. "You know, not all businesses allow dogs inside their doors."

"I know."

His face twisted, the same disgust taking up residence. "Next time, perhaps you could leave him at home."

"Or perhaps I just won't frequent the businesses where my dog isn't allowed."

And with that, I strolled outside and let the door close behind me, separating Corbin and me once more. I took a deep, head-clearing breath before heading for my van with a burning knot in my chest. I really hoped that was the last time I had to deal with Corbin Lamb. I knew I hadn't liked the man, but the fact that he openly hated my dog cemented that. The fact that I didn't think he was the thief felt like a lost opportunity—the man made one heck of a villain.

"C'mon, Elmer," I said once I had the passenger door open. "Let's play hooky from the store, go back home to the manor, and see what sort of trouble we can get into on all that land."

Chapter Fifteen

When I pulled into the driveway at the manor, I got the surprise of the week. Mike Allen—delivery driver and suspect in my search for manor thief—stood on my porch. Not just waiting on the porch like most people might if they found themselves knocking on an unanswered door but looking through the windows of the house with a package in his hand. Ruse or actual delivery? Time to find out.

"Mike?" I let Elmer out of the van before heading for the front of the house. "What are you doing here?"

"Hey, Miss Brylie." The man waved, looking decidedly awkward but not at all threatening. Which could have been an act. "I saw that you had a package at the post office and thought I'd bring it by. I don't think anyone over there knows who you are yet."

He just so happened to see a package addressed to me at the post office? Like what...out on the counter? Small towns were kooky in an annoying sort of way but that seemed unsafe.

"Thanks," I said, trying hard to keep a smile on my face

and forcing my anxiety to quiet down. "Would you like to come in? I've got lemonade in the fridge."

Mike grinned. "I'd love to, if you have the time. I haven't been out here in a long while."

Maybe...maybe not. I unlocked the door and headed inside, with Elmer trotting right behind me. Okay, maybe not trotting. Just sort of...plodding. Whatever. The dog didn't seem bothered in the least by the man walking into the house. In fact, Elmer headed straight to his favorite spot at the bottom of the stairs and plopped. Snoring would begin in three...two...

"Wow. He really does fall asleep fast," Mike said, watching the dog as I ran to wipe up the leak in the hallway. The one that shouldn't have been there.

"Jealous?"

Mike huffed a quiet laugh. "Aren't we all?"

Yes. Yes, we were.

I finished with the water—my kingdom for a house that stayed dry for just one day—before indicating he should follow me. I led Mike down the squeakiest hallway ever to the kitchen, where I really did have a pitcher of fresh lemonade in the refrigerator. I washed my hands before getting to work, pouring glasses of lemonade and arranging cookies on an actual plate instead of in the compostable takeout container they'd come home in. I had become a right Martha Stewart.

"Have a cookie," I said as I set the plate on the counter. Sitting at the table felt too formal, but standing around the island seemed right. Mike must have agreed because he seemed to have no trouble following my lead.

"Are these the ones from the diner?" Mike asked as he looked over the cookies.

"Yeah, Ander hired some new, local baker to supply

desserts for the diner. He must have bought too many because he sent me home with a box."

Mike's smile turned a little wicked and teasing. "He must really like you. He never sends me home with cookies."

I was far too old to blush, but boy did I want to. Of course I'd realized Ander was paying a bit more attention to me than to his other diners and that he seemed to spoil me a little. The man had made his interest known. That didn't mean the whole town had to know about us, did it? I wasn't ready to answer *that* question or talk about Ander in any capacity other than him as the local chef and business owner. Thankfully, Mike didn't push the issue or leave us in one of those awkward silences.

"The place looks nice," he said, glancing around. "Had some leaks, though, huh?"

Some was an understatement. "Yeah. The whole place was soaked when I first got here, but I think I've got everything mostly under control now."

"Except the hallway."

I nodded. "Except the hallway. I'll get it fixed eventually, but the leak seems to be really minor, so it's not something to lose sleep over."

"Frustrating to not be able to find the cause."

"Exactly. I keep thinking I'm going to walk into another flood every time I open the door."

"I hear you. I just bought a house, and the hot water heater keeps going out on me. I cross my fingers every time I walk inside that I'll have hot water in the taps instead of fifty gallons of it soaking my basement floor."

Sometimes, I couldn't help but be a hardware store owner. "I can order you a new one, you know."

"I know, and if I could, I'd definitely buy one from you."

He grimaced, looking a little uncomfortable. "Money's tight right now, though."

My spidey senses pinged—*money was tight*. Tight enough to turn to a life of crime to supplement his income? And who said *life if crime* anymore? I really needed to stop the dramatics inside my head.

"Well, you let me know. I'm here to help."

"Thanks. I appreciate it." He shook his head, still smiling. "You and your aunt Gwen are so much alike."

Which was a subject change I hadn't been prepared for. "How's that?"

"Kind. Gwen was so excited when I bought my house, so supportive. She and Rose had already told me so much in terms of fixing things and what to look out for. Hot water heater aside, I got a great house at a low price because of what they taught me. I don't know what I would have done without them over the years."

My heart jumped a little. This kid—and he was really a kid—seemed honestly sweet and caring. He seemed as if he'd truly liked Rose and still wanted to be in Aunt Gwen's life. But was *sweet* enough to keep him from fleecing the women? He'd said money was tight; were his own desires enough to make his morals take a break so he could steal what he needed? How could I tell?

Man. Trying to solve a mystery was hard.

"Yeah," I said, refocusing on the conversation and trying to think of a way to redirect it toward something helpful. I mean, asking *"By the way, did you happen to pop over yesterday in a ski mask?"* didn't seem conducive to fostering a sense of trust and open communication. "I'm sad that I never met Rose, but Aunt Gwen is the best. I'm really happy she found me."

"You didn't know her?"

I shook my head, wrapping my hands a little tighter around my sweating glass. "My mom died when I was little, and my dad had no family. I always assumed there was no one but him and me left."

"So, how did Miss Gwen find you?"

Now that someone asked... "I'm not really sure. My dad died a few months back—"

"I'm so sorry for your loss." Mike reached out and patted my arm, an almost awkward sort of touch, but one I appreciated.

"Thanks. It was really sudden. After he died, I received a phone call from this woman claiming to be my great-aunt. Bim, bam, boom, I now live in Reverie Springs and own the manor."

"And the hardware store."

I nodded. "And the hardware store. Which reminds me—have you ever been there on hexing day?"

Mike laughed—all out, head back, loud as heck laughed. "Seriously, Gwen is the best. That potion she brews? It will keep everyone away."

Of that, I had no doubt. "Wonderful."

"But just wait. Her love potions smell like warm cookies or something. The entire town will come to the store on those days."

I had to give myself a few seconds to let those words sink in because, on first listen, they didn't seem to make any sense. "She brews love potions too?"

Mike shifted his weight and dropped his gaze to the counter, looking decidedly uncomfortable. "I mean...she brews whatever someone needs. And sometimes, a person needs a little help. You know. With like...romance and stuff. Not like, anything controlling or...you know. Just like...a little request from the universe. To move faster. Or something."

Oh, his stumbling and how dark his neck had gotten were positively delicious giveaways. I couldn't hold back my grin. "Did you have Aunt Gwen brew you a love potion?"

He coughed and raised his lemonade glass, finishing the contents in one fell swoop before finally answering in a quiet voice. "There aren't a lot of dating options in Reverie Springs."

Oh. Yeah. I could see that. "I'm not making fun of you or blaming you. I'm more curious about the whole process. I've never met anyone who brews hexes and potions before."

"Neither had I until I met Miss Gwen. I never would have believed anyone else if they'd come at me with that stuff either. I'll tell you what, though—all you need to do is watch her go about town on hexing day, and you'll be a convert."

"Does she make magic happen?"

"No. She scares the whole town. Whatever is in that stinky stuff, people are afraid of it, which makes them treat her with more respect and kindness than they might have without the threat of being hexed looming over them. Now *that's* power."

"And the love potions?"

He shrugged, a small smile tugging up one side of his mouth. "I took the potion on the full moon as she directed, and a week later, I met my girlfriend."

"Could be a coincidence."

"Could be, or it could be that the potion gave me the confidence to approach a pretty girl I normally wouldn't have had the guts to talk to. Either way, I got the girl." He gave me a grin. "The end justifies the means, you know?"

"Not always," I said with an exaggerated eye roll. Deep down, though, my stomach had twisted because those words... there was a wrongness to them. I liked Mike. He seemed sweet and funny, easy to talk to. But that line—the end justifying the means—sat wrong with me. That could be applied to anything in life—speeding to get where you were going faster, driving drunk because making it home was more important than another person's safety, or stealing architectural elements from an old, abandoned house because you needed the money more than the woman who owned the place and had left it to rot. And yet, I had no sense of ill will from him. No sniff of negative energy. Not a single itch of a lie. My doubt was high that he would steal from me.

Before I could really sink into my thoughts on that topic, a loud clang sounded from my freezer. One I'd been hearing for days.

"Shoot," I said, jumping up and running to grab a towel. "Stupid ice maker."

Mike hurried over to help. "What's wrong with it?"

I didn't even have to answer because within seconds, the floor grew wet with a flood of water seeping from under the fridge.

"Oh," he said. "I bet you need a new filter."

"Yeah, that was my thought. I replaced the main water line because it was corroded, but I had thought the filter and final tubing to the unit were good." I grabbed another towel, tucking it as far under the appliance as I could to hopefully keep the floors from any further damage. "Guess I was wrong."

"You got the parts here?"

"Sure do. I just hadn't had the time to fix it yet, plus the filter is in a weird spot. It's hard to reach, and I have to move the entire refrigerator to access the connections."

Mike shrugged. "I've got some time."

I blinked, the entire world skipping like a record scratch. "You'd help me?"

"Of course. What are friends for?"

Friends. I wasn't sure I would call him a friend just yet, seeing as how I was still wondering if he had been breaking in to my house almost on the nightly, but I'd take his help.

The end justified the means, right?

"Let me just grab my toolbox."

Chapter Sixteen

The next morning—after another night of sleeping in my cramped minivan—I left Willow Manor behind and headed into town for a full day at the hardware store. I still had so much work to do before I could even consider opening the doors to the public, but the house had slipped into my main priority. Perhaps not the smartest move, considering I needed the income from the store to fix up the house, but I simply couldn't help myself. Something about the home seemed so... sad. The very walls radiated a constant sense of loss and anguish. Of pain.

Or perhaps I had been deflecting my own grief on to an inanimate object to keep from dealing with emotions I wasn't ready to face just yet.

"Nah, that can't be it."

"What can't be what?" Aunt Gwendolyn swept into the diner where I'd taken up residence to grab a decent lunch—and further avoid my responsibilities next door. Her floaty garments were a deep, dark gray today. She looked like...well, sort of like a ghost in a lot of ways. The color fit her, though. As did the spider rings on her fingers.

"Just talking to myself. Nice jewelry choice." I nodded toward her hand. "Trying to scare off some kids before you need to hex them?"

"Are you afraid of spiders?" She took the seat across from me and held up her hand, twisting it so the gems making up the spider body glittered in the lights. "You shouldn't be. They have a dark side, of course, but they are bringers of light and filled with the feminine energy."

"Feeling particularly feminine today?"

"No—creative. I was thinking of painting later, and spiders have always been bearers of creativity for me. I was hoping wearing these would inspire me." She smiled as Ander himself approached the table. "Good afternoon, Ander. Could I get a Cobb salad and an iced tea, please?"

Ander nodded, looking my way. "Enjoying the special?"

The special was a large serving of chicken fried steak over mashed potatoes with a side of fresh green beans. I was in heaven with it. "Definitely, though it's way too much food. I'm going to have to take half home with me."

He nodded, a small smile kind of pulling up one side of his mouth. If the wiggle of his beard was any indication, at least. "Let me know when you're finished, and I'll box it up for you."

"Thanks, Ander." I watched him walk away, admiring the view. How could I not? The man had shoulders wide enough to block a doorway. Not that I should have been looking—I had enough on my plate without adding romantic entanglements to the mix. Besides, he'd said to let him know when my maybe had firmed up into a yes. I wasn't there yet.

"Enjoying the view?" Aunt Gwendolyn asked, grabbing my attention and shooting me a wink.

Caught. Time to refocus on the woman across from me. "Nothing wrong with looking. Back to the subject at hand, though—I didn't know you were an artist."

She cocked her head, looking at me with those light, knowing eyes that made me feel way too much. Things I shouldn't feel at all. "Of course not, dear Brylie. You barely know me at all, do you?"

Something in her tone, in the emotions she held at bay, made my stomach clench and my heart beat too fast. Right —I barely knew her. And yet, it felt as if I'd known her my entire life. As if I had felt her energy before and understood where she was coming from before she had to tell me. I may have only just met her, but I knew her soul. Somehow.

The appearance of Ander at the table again stole my attention. The man seemed tired...and way more present than usual.

"No Mary today?" I asked.

"She had to register her daughter for preschool, so I'm running the front and back of house until she can get here." He frowned, looking under the table. "Speaking of children, where's Elmer?"

"I left him at the hardware store. He was super cranky from spending all day yesterday guarding me, dealing with deliveries from Mike, and being reluctantly allowed into Corbin Lamb's office."

"Corbin?" It was Aunt Gwen's turn to frown. "What were you doing there?"

"Trying to find out why he wants me to sell the manor so badly."

Her face went white, and she gripped the edge of the table. The energy in the room shifted quickly, moving from basic and nondescript to stressed, bordering on fear and anger. "You want to sell the manor?"

"No," I said, recognizing the need to calm her down. "Not at all. But he really wants me to, and I find his interest in the house odd. Particularly since so much stuff has gone missing."

"Still having trouble out there?" Ander asked, a wave of anger vibrating between us. His anger. I'd thought it had been coming from Aunt Gwendolyn, but apparently I'd been wrong.

"I mean..." I swallowed and shrugged, suddenly feeling like a bug under a magnifying glass. "I'm handling it."

"Have you called anyone for help?" he asked. Likely not meaning him since he knew I hadn't called him.

I shook my head. "The sheriff isn't helpful, so I'm trying to deal with whoever keeps breaking in on my own."

"That sounds dangerous."

"I've got Elmer. He's a good alarm system."

Ander didn't look convinced.

"So, what did you find out from Corbin?" Aunt Gwendolyn asked, bringing the conversation back around before taking a bite of her salad.

"He says the value's in the land. He wants to subdivide the property so a developer can build new neighborhoods there and then sell the house separately."

Aunt Gwendolyn huffed. "Rose would turn over in her grave."

And Gwen would likely never forgive me because she'd also owned the manor—not that I was supposed to know that. I reached across the table and placed my hand over hers, the cold stones of the spider rings biting into my fingers. "I wouldn't do that to you or to her memory. The manor is not for sale—not the house or the land. I promise."

She sat back, seemingly much more comfortable. The anxiousness in the air dissipating. "Thank you."

As if she needed to thank me. "Ander, I think I'm done with my lunch. If you want to bring me a box—"

He grabbed the plate, shaking his head. His anger still making itself known. "I'll take care of it."

My throat tightened at his clipped response, the harshness in his voice making me feel as if I'd done something wrong. As if my talking about selling the manor—even though I had been explicit in the fact that I would not—had bothered him. Or maybe he was concerned that I had been dealing with the thief all on my own.

Concern intrigued me. Even if I didn't need his help, I would have liked having it. Maybe. Perhaps. If I didn't have to ask for it.

Aunt Gwendolyn waited for Ander to disappear into the kitchen before leaning closer, refocusing my attention on her. "Do you think Corbin is the one breaking in to the manor?"

Do I? Did I? Had I ever? Ugh. "I don't. Not really. He doesn't seem like the type to be willing to get his hands dirty."

She nodded. "Yes. He always was a bit...lazy in that regard."

"I'm not ready to say he definitely isn't the one, I just don't think he's working alone if he's involved. No way would he have pulled that mantel all by himself. I don't think it's Mike either. The kid is just so nice, and I don't get any sort of malevolent intentions off him."

"Malevolent? That's a five-dollar word."

"It is, but it gets the point across."

"Very true. So, no Corbin, no Mike...that leaves Joan and Thomas on the list of possibilities, though neither seems very likely to me."

I sighed. "Agreed. I feel as if we're missing something, but I can't figure out what."

Aunt Gwendolyn looked up and smiled as a harried-looking Mary rushed into the dining room. "Good afternoon, Mary. Get little Louise all ready for school?"

Mary huffed but grinned. "I did, though they certainly don't make it easy on working parents to deal with these things. Registration from eleven until two? That's prime time for my job." She glanced toward the kitchen. "Did he seem okay while I was gone?"

"He was fine, dear," Aunt Gwen said with a wink in my direction. "He had his favorite customer here."

Two days in a row that I'd felt the need to blush even though I was far too old for it. "Stop that."

"What?" Aunt Gwendolyn asked, looking forcefully innocent. "He doesn't offer to box up anyone else's unfinished food."

So maybe he didn't. That didn't mean...anything other than he was being nice to me. Really nice. There was nothing wrong with nice.

Unless that nice came from a beast of a man with eyes as black as coal and a beard that hid his facial expressions to the point that he seemed like the grumpiest soul ever at first and then sort of...melted into a huge teddy bear of a human.

I always had liked teddy bears.

A thought that sent my heart racing a little too much.

"I have to go," I said, bolting to my feet. "I need to check on Elmer."

Aunt Gwendolyn and Mary both looked at me as if I'd suddenly grown horns.

"Don't rush off on my account," Mary said.

I shook my head, my insides all topsy-turvy and my

emotions flickering like some sort of dying light bulb. Feelings I'd never really wanted to explore making themselves known. At the exact wrong time for them. "It's not you. I just don't like leaving Elmer alone for long. He tends to get into trouble when I do. I'll see you ladies tomorrow, okay?"

And with that, I rushed out the door and jogged to the hardware store, unlocking the back door and rushing inside before I could stop myself. Elmer met me at the door, still annoyed and definitely even more mad at me for leaving him by himself. He didn't look dirty or as if he'd gotten into anything, though. Bonus for me.

"What do you think, buddy?" I asked, trying hard to settle the storm inside myself. "Want to work here or head home and see if we can get that wallpaper to stick to the walls?"

Elmer didn't answer, but he didn't need to. I wanted to be at the manor. Something inside me didn't want to be locked in the store all day, and I had gotten really good over the years at listening to my instincts. It was time to leave.

So, we did.

I spent the afternoon and evening on a ladder in the hallway, carefully attempting to reapply the wallpaper that had fallen over the years. The process was delicate and time-consuming, requiring every single bit of my attention. Exactly what I needed after the few days I'd had. Between Corbin Lamb, Mike Allen, and Ander, I wanted to give my brain time to noodle over the issues at hand before I made any plans for my next move. Keeping my hands busy and my thoughts focused was a good way to let my subconscious do just that. Noodle.

It was close to nine when I finally called it a night and headed for the minivan. I dreaded another night in the thing, but I still didn't feel safe enough to stay inside the house alone.

Still didn't want to leave myself open for attack without backup. Not counting Elmer, of course.

I had just settled onto the seat when lights suddenly shone through the windows and an engine rumbled closer. Someone had turned onto my driveway. Elmer barked at the door as if demanding I open it, which seemed both idiotic and the only logical choice at the moment.

"Not like we can hide in here," I said. I jumped up and scampered out of the van, Elmer leading the way across the gravel drive. My dog seemed excited, but wasn't barking or growling. In fact, he stood in the light and wagged his tail as the vehicle crept closer.

"You know this person, Elmer?"

He barked and hurried forward as a truck stopped behind my van and the driver's side door opened. Yeah, Elmer knew the driver. So did I—knew him and the warm energy that came with him.

"Ander?" I stepped closer, wrapping my arms around myself. I didn't sleep in pajamas per se, but flannel shorts and a tank top were a little more intimate than what I'd normally be dressed in for company. "What are you doing here?"

He held up a large paper bag. "You forgot your food."

My leftovers. From lunch. My stomach nearly growled at the idea of that chicken fried steak. "You deliver now?"

"For you, yes." He shrugged. "Sorry I'm so late. I had to wait for the dinner rush to end, and we had a party that refused to leave." His face twisted, eyebrows dropping and beard showing definite signs of movement. "What are you doing in your van?"

As much as I hated to admit my reality to him, I felt as if I had to. So, I did.

"I sleep in there."

Ander's eyebrows flew up, his surprise slamming into me like a wave of emotion. "Why do you do that?"

I never had been one to lie—mostly because it gave me hives. Even if it didn't though, lying to Ander seemed almost too far over the line of right versus wrong to even consider. "Because I'm too afraid of someone breaking in to sleep inside."

"You've been sleeping in your van all this time?"

"Yes."

"Why didn't you ask for help?"

"Help sleeping?"

He huffed, handing me the bag. "Get in the van and don't do anything."

"Like what?"

"Just get in the van and stay put. I mean it."

I did as I was told, settling in and locking the doors as Ander...well, as he left. He didn't even say goodbye. But I listened to his last demand for reasons I couldn't explain. I stayed put. In fact, I sat there in that minivan staring out the windows for what had to be twenty minutes, sulking a bit. At minute twenty-one, the headlights were back, though. I stepped out of the van just in time to see Ander hop down from his truck with a duffel bag in hand.

"I told you to stay in there."

My eyes couldn't roll any harder than they did. "I stayed until you came back. That counts." I pointed at his bag. "What's that?"

"My stuff." He reached into the back of the truck and pulled out a cooler—one of those bigger ones that could fit a whole thanksgiving meal in it. Not like one for a six-pack—the man had come prepared for something.

I really wanted to know what that thing was. "What are you doing?"

He didn't even pause, striding for the porch with purpose. "Moving in."

It took me way too long to catch up to him...and to be able to process those words. "Why?"

"Because if you're too stubborn to see reason and ask for help, then I'll just have to override you. I'm here to protect you."

The independent side of me lit the fuse and set my temper on fire. "I don't need protecting."

"Bull," he said as he walked right past me and up the stairs to the porch.

I was more than a little embarrassed to be chasing after him, I had to be honest. I did, though. Right up the stairs and across the wooden floor to the front door. "Bull? Just bull?"

"Yeah, just bull." He stopped, glaring down at me, a swirl of emotions too drowned out by my own to identify. "You've been sleeping in your car."

"So?"

"So, that means you're afraid, and I'm not okay with that."

"Why do you care?"

He set the cooler down, those eyebrows furrowed deep. "Why do I care?"

"Yeah...why do you care? Are you just going to keep repeating my questions now?"

He shook his head and dropped his bag, stepping around the cooler and into my space. "No. I'm going to do this."

The next thing I knew, Ander had his lips on mine with his arms wrapped around me so tight, I couldn't have taken a breath if I'd tried. Not that I needed to. The moment his flesh touched mine, that he made the move to join us, breathing became inconsequential. I didn't need air; I just needed him. His body pressing against mine. His scent drowning me. The feel of his warmth against me.

I wasn't mad about about Ander inserting himself into my situation. I needed Ander kissing me more than anything else out there.

When he finally broke the kiss, I took a few seconds to recenter myself and stop thinking about lips and kisses and how warm Ander felt. Took a quiet moment to bask in the feeling of joy building between us, of connection. Of being able to have help without having to ask for it from a man who kissed like *that*.

I may have taken more than just a moment, though.

"Brylie?" Ander's voice came out rough but quiet. A sound I wanted to hear again and again. Just not on my porch.

"Fine," I said, taking a step back. Pulling away from him and avoiding the temptation of more kisses. "You can stay. But we'll be sleeping in separate sleeping bags."

"As I assumed."

I opened the front door to let him in, moving aside as he twisted to carry the cooler across the threshold. "Is that food in there? Are you going to cook for me?"

Ander grunted in the affirmative. "Of course I'm going to cook for you—a late dinner so you can have the leftovers for lunch. Tomorrow, breakfast will need to be at the diner because of the Sunday rush, but I'll make you dinner out here again since the restaurant isn't open past lunch."

The two of us all alone in the diner. Alone. Just us. "Is this...are we going on a date?"

"Are we?"

I sighed, unable to keep from pulling back. "Please don't just repeat my question."

Ander froze, those dark eyes locking on mine. His sincerity screaming through the air around me. "Fine. Yes. It's a date."

I closed the front door, leaning back against it. Needing a little more space between him and me. "You didn't ask me to go on a date with you."

He shrugged. "I didn't think I needed to."

Of course he didn't, because I'd been about ready to climb him like a tree right there on my front porch. "A woman likes to be asked out, you know."

He set the cooler down again, staring at me hard, that beard moving in the way that I assumed meant he was smiling. Inching closer and surrounding me with that typical Ander warmth. "Hey, Brylie?"

"Yeah," I gasped, nearly shaking under his dark gaze.

"Will you go on a date with me?"

The world slipped away, the tension and worries and pressure gone. The only thing in my orbit was Ander and me and opportunities for time together.

"Brylie," Ander said, that deep grumble almost threatening and tugging a smile from me.

"Right," I said, taking a deep breath. "Will I go on a date with you?"

"Woman—"

Gosh, this was fun. "Fine. Yes. I will definitely go on a date with you."

If I hadn't known better, I'd have said the house herself sighed in a feminine sort of relief.

Ander chuckled and picked up the cooler, heading for the kitchen at the back of the house. "I was worried there for a second. You're going to drive me to drink something harder than water or soda."

"Well, this is the right house for that."

He paused, looking over his shoulder at me. "What do you mean?"

"It's so wet here."

Ander looked around, his brow heavily furrowed. "Wet?"

I moved to point to the spot where the powder room bathroom always leaked, but I noticed that for the first time since I'd stepped into Willow Manor, there was no standing water in the foyer. Not a single puddle or drop. The floor was shockingly, perfectly dry.

Chapter Seventeen

For the first time in a month, I awoke without a crick in my neck, a pain in my back, or a Basset hound barking to be let out of the minivan. I almost felt like an entirely new woman with just one good night's sleep.

I found a note next to me on the family room couch where Ander and I had bunked for the night. Not together, really—I took one side, he took the other. There were no shenanigans. He had refused to leave me alone in a room, and I had refused to let him sleep on the floor. Thankfully, the family room couch had been comfortable enough for us to sleep on and had given us room to spread out. Plus, I didn't really need a bed—the couch was enough of an upgrade from the minivan for my first night inside.

Bliss. Sleeping on something soft was pure bliss.

Elmer huffed and half jumped up onto the couch, his front legs landing on the paper. Note. Right. I tugged the white square from under Elmer's front paw and squinted at the scratchy handwriting.

I had to leave to open the diner but didn't want to wake you.

There's coffee in the carafe, some muffins on the counter, and Elmer has been fed. I'll lock the front door behind me. See you tonight—don't try to talk me out of staying again. Ander.

So it was just Elmer and me. Alone in the manor.

Somehow, the idea didn't scare me as much as it had. Not anymore, at least.

Two cups of coffee, a muffin, and a hot shower later, Elmer and I were doing what we normally did when home alone. Dealing with water.

"I really don't know what to do," I said to my sidekick as I wiped the floor outside the half bath where, once again, a puddle had appeared. "There's nothing wrong with the pipes. Nothing. All the connections are solid, the toilet tank isn't leaking, and there's absolutely no reason why there should be water out here. There wasn't water last night when we came inside with Ander, and yet—" I swung my arm, indicating the floor "—here we are. Again."

The house groaned long and loud, almost as if trying to tell me something. As if talking to me. Not that *that* was a possibility. Of course, neither was the water standing right there in front of me, so...fine, the house was talking to me.

"I would really like for the leaking to stop," I said aloud. I swiped at the last of the water, sighing once the floor looked dry again. "Please. No more water."

A creak behind me made me jump, but I had been getting used to the old house. That had been a settling sort of noise. Out of place and oddly coincidental, but normal. Or as normal as anything in Reverie Springs and especially Willow Manor seemed to be.

"What do you think, Elmer? Did that work?"

Elmer huffed from where he sat across the hall as if affronted by my interrupting his rest. Not that he should have been tired this morning. He wasn't much into the working part of my day, but he certainly seemed to have liked sleeping indoors again. His snoring had even woken me up once or twice.

Snoring made me think of sleeping, and sleeping made me think of Ander and...well, I didn't think Ander had snored at all last night. Or if he had, I'd slept through it. Which seemed odd to me and yet not at the same time—I hadn't ever slept in the same room as a man who wasn't my father, so I hadn't been sure what to expect. Would he snore? Would he kick or roll a lot? Would he try something in the quiet and the dark of night?

I should have known better. Ander had been a complete gentleman, of course. He had stayed not to take advantage of a situation, but to keep us safe. Keep us safe and feed us—that seemed to be Ander's mission.

And mine appeared to be cleaning up water.

Just after lunch, Aunt Gwendolyn showed up. She came prancing into the house, her energy high and her smile bright. Her clothing didn't match her mood, something that I'd begun to notice with all the time we spent together. The woman always wore gray or black—no colors. It seemed intentional.

"You're looking awfully chipper today," I said as I leaned on the mop that had become like a sentinel in the foyer. "What's the occasion?"

Aunt Gwendolyn shrugged, her silvery blouse rising and falling with the motion. Beyond the question about her color palette, I had one other thing I really wanted to know—how did she get her clothing to dance like that?

"I figured it was time to brighten things up around here."

I cocked my head, my eyebrow rising almost of its own volition. "Brighten them up how?"

She practically skipped right past me, giving me a secret

sort of smile as she did. "We're going to bring a few things back to life."

"I'm not big on the whole resurrection thing normally, so if there are some dead pets buried in the backyard, you can leave them there."

"Not pets, Brylie. Come. Spend some time with an old woman."

As if I didn't do that almost daily.

We ended up in the conservatory—a glass-walled building off the kitchen. It looked a lot like a greenhouse to me, especially with all the planting pots sitting around on the benches. There was also a large display cabinet with carved headers and glass doors along the only solid wall in the place. One holding a multitude of bottles and jars with handwritten labels. One I had been ignoring for fear of what the heck was in there.

Aunt Gwendolyn immediately headed to the cabinet. "A lot of this will have gone bad over the years, but there may be some special surprises in here."

I had a feeling there might be some sort of nasty strain of fungus in there that would devour us all, but I kept my mouth shut about that. She seemed truly happy. Comfortable and calm as she opened the glass doors and started pulling bottles down. Her hands moved deftly from item to item, her eyes scanning each label. She seemed to be making two segments, though what the difference was between them, I had no idea. She had also started humming softly to herself, something I wouldn't have paid much attention to except for the fact that the house...

Well, the house seemed to be humming back at her.

The shift in the energy of the place was subtle, but once I noticed it, denial felt impossible. Everything appeared just a little brighter somehow, as if I'd cleaned all the windows in the room and allowed the sunlight to stream in. The overall vibe of the space turned positive, too. Every worry I usually felt, every bit of sadness that seemed to lurk in the shadows, had vanished with Aunt Gwendolyn's arrival. I hadn't even realized how depressing being inside the manor had been until it no longer was.

But the manor's humming was something else entirely. Something I had never once in my life experienced. It wasn't as if the heating system had turned on or an appliance buzzed somewhere in the background. No. This was more of a sense of wind against the windows or a breeze dancing past the eaves. Not a true sound, a feeling. This humming was light and airy, the sound of an average day passing us by without a worry weighing us down. The sound of life both inside and outside the walls.

It took me several minutes to place my finger on what I was experiencing, but when I did, there was no holding back my conclusion.

"The house is happy you're here."

Aunt Gwendolyn turned slowly, a slight smile on her face. "And I'm happy to be here as well. She's a good, old house. She'll treat you well if you let her."

Her response only fueled more questions, her simple understanding giving me the green light to be curious. "How can a house feel happy?"

"The manor isn't just your average house, Brylie." The woman's smile grew, something close to satisfaction dancing in her eyes. "And you're not just an average woman, are you? You feel things deeply, things you shouldn't be able to feel. Things no one else can."

I should have seen the conversation turning back to me. I

really should have. My throat tightened as I answered her. "My dad always told me I was too sensitive."

"Your dad, bless his soul, was wrong. He was also a bit closed-minded to the Laveau family gifts." She shook her head, sighing. "What your mother saw in him, I'll never know."

I bristled, grief thumping at my temper. "He was a good man, and they were happy together, that's what."

Those pale eyes darted to mine, and she nodded. "Of course they were. I'm not trying to diminish their happiness, but he never let her be her true self. She had to try to be normal for him—had to let go of our history and talents. She chose to do that, though, so she must have really loved him."

"And he loved *her*. He never even dated after she died."

Every bit of happiness swept out of the room, ushering in a heavy, weighted sort of energy that seemed to smother me. Aunt Gwendolyn stared my way, looking ready to cry, as if overcome with an emotion too strong to hold back. I could see it...and sense it. Deep pain lived within her. Pure agony.

I couldn't let it go. "That hurts you."

She nodded, still holding my gaze. Still sending me her feelings. "Losing your mother hurt me deeply."

An uncomfortable sensation washed over me. Not a true itchiness like when someone lied. This wasn't nearly as strong or irritating. This was more of a general sort of uncomfortableness. Aunt Gwendolyn wasn't lying, but she wasn't telling the whole truth either.

Before I could ask her about that, though, she sighed and reached for my hand. "My child, when we ignore our gifts, they die. Just like the plants in this room."

I glanced over her shoulder at the shelves and tables around the wall of windows. At the empty pots and dirty panes of glass. I took in every nook and cranny of the space as the energy lightened once more.

And as I stated the obvious. "There are no plants in here."

She smiled, a simple yet wicked sort of expression, before taking our joined hands and holding them over what looked to me like a pot of old, dry dirt. Something warm washed over me, something comfortable and familiar and yet totally new. The energy in the air grew brighter and stronger as each second passed, and what felt like a slight breeze skittered past us. The entire house suddenly felt as if there was magic in the air.

"Aunt Gwendo—"

"Seven generations of Laveau women have lived in Reverie Springs. We have brought magic to the people here. Your mother chose to leave us, which was her right to do. It left a hole, though. A gaping wound in the area that turned the energy from one of peace to something less stable. But you've come back so the energy can be reignited. The balance restored. The magic resurrected."

And as I stood there, my hand joined with hers, that pot of old, dry dirt changed. The dryness...went away. The color deepened and the texture loosened. And as the energy sizzled, as it intensified between us, one single little green thread appeared. It grew thicker and longer, the slow change from nothing to something fascinating to me. This was pure magic, for sure. And it was glorious.

"If we stop," Aunt Gwen said, focusing on the plant. "If we let go of our magic, the gift dies. The next generation won't know about the energy in the world or how to control it. They won't understand the history of our family. You've come back to Reverie Springs. Now come back to your magic."

"I don't have any magic." But even as I said the words, I

knew they were a lie. The feelings, the senses of other peoples' emotions, the way I just knew how they were feeling.

"Have you figured it out yet?" Aunt Gwendolyn's voice slipped over my skin and into my very soul, reaching somewhere and calling out to something that I hadn't known existed. Awakening something that had always been asleep.

I couldn't decide if I should be excited or terrified to admit what I knew I'd been hiding my entire life. To accept my place. "I've always known."

"Yes, you have," Aunt Gwendolyn said, her voice soft but hopeful. Light but filled with power. "You're a witch, darling. Just like your mom and me and our ancestors before us. That power simmers under your skin. Your witch is ready to be let loose."

I took a deep breath and focused on the one thing I knew about her style of witchcraft. "Am I going to have to brew stinky potions and hex people?"

She laughed. "Not if you don't want to. I get the feeling your gift lies a bit outside the realm of spellwork. I think you already know this, though."

I did. I always had, even though I had been trying to deny it. Trying to hide it. There would be no more hiding, it seemed. "I *feel* things."

"You do. I believe you're an empath. Much like your mother was."

I darted a look in her direction, unable not to. "She felt things like I do?"

"Yes. It's what made her so special. She had a way of knowing how people were feeling and would do her best to help them. A smile, a laugh, a shared moment of irritation...she balanced her gifts well."

"But she knew about them her entire life. She accepted that

part of herself?" Because I hadn't known—not really. I'd always noticed something was different in how I perceived the world, but my dad had told me to keep that part of myself quiet. To push it down. And I had. How different my childhood might have been had my mother survived and been there to guide me.

A thought that dimmed even the brightness of a happy house.

"She did. But don't worry, child. You'll pick it up quickly once you stop trying to block it. I have faith in you." Aunt Gwendolyn dropped my hand, picking up the little pot and bringing it toward her face as she inspected the new sprout there. Smiling at our work. "And in this plant. I do believe this little bit of energy is done for the day. They'll be growing strong and hearty, though. Just don't forget to water them."

"I've got enough of that around here."

Aunt Gwendolyn looked about ready to ask me a question, but her eyes darted to something over my shoulder. "Ah, Carl is out back. He must be looking for Thomas."

Thomas—the farmer. The one suspect I hadn't gotten to interact much with yet. But someone Aunt Gwendolyn did.

"Did Rose like Thomas?"

"She did, very much. He was a good friend to her."

"And Carl?"

Aunt Gwen laughed. "For sure. Those two had quite the weekly poker game. They'd invite half the town over to put their money down. It was a roaring good time. At least until the mill closed."

Without thought, without really planning out what I was going to say, I opened my mouth and... "I know you used to live here. You and Rose both lived in the manor."

Aunt Gwendolyn stopped, staring at another empty pot. Reaching out to touch the dirt. Another plant came to life, fast this time, as if energized by her touch. A flower blooming from nothing. A single red rose forming...then withering right there on the stem.

"We did, yes."

The tone of her voice warned me to tread carefully; the shift in energy around her, the dimming of the lights, reinforced that. This was a delicate topic. "You two must have been really good friends."

"We were. She was the best person I've ever met."

My body reacted to her words, that uncomfortable buzz back on my skin. Not a lie but not the truth either. Something still hidden.

Carefully. Tread carefully. "Why didn't you tell me?"

She set the little rose stem down, tucking the fallen petals into the dirt with a sigh. "Some stories are simply too hard to tell."

I cocked my head, focusing on the emotions coming my way. Reading them as best I could. "Why do you feel guilty?"

Aunt Gwendolyn shot me a sad sort of smile. "See? Your gift comes back once you begin to use it. I dare say you might be a stronger empath than your mother was."

"Don't change the subject, old lady."

She sighed. "I have a lot of guilt where Rose is concerned, mostly because of her death." Those light eyes met mine, the edges rimmed in red. "I was with her in the car the night of the accident. I survived, but she didn't."

My heart dropped as understanding washed over me. "Aunt Gwen—"

"There was nothing I could do—no potions or spells could heal the sort of damage she endured. I called the sheriff, but we're too far outside the city around here, so it took time for them to get to us." She stared out the window as the sky darkened further, as everything around us seemed to become covered in storm clouds. As her sadness took on a physical sort of form. "I had to watch her die on the side of the road while I waited for help to arrive. I was completely powerless."

Like my dad had been when my mother had died in a different car accident. Like I had been when my father's heart had suddenly stopped beating right there in front of me. The universe had a way of throwing obstacles into our paths to remind us that we were not invincible. That there was nothing we could do to stop her if she decided the end had come for something...or someone.

Aunt Gwendolyn and I were much more alike than I would have guessed.

"This was supposed to be a happy day," Aunt Gwendolyn said, taking a deep breath and seeming to brush off the sadness that had blanketed her. "I think it's time for dinner. Let's get out of this old girl and head into town."

As much as I hated leaving the conversation unfinished and ignoring the questions that still needed to be answered, emotions needed time to rest after such a workout.

Except... "Ander is supposed to come out and make me dinner."

"He won't mind an old lady spending time with her only family. I'll send him a note right now." She pulled her phone from her pocket. Determined. Not waiting for me to answer her.

Wouldn't have mattered, anyway—I wasn't about to tell her no. Besides, a girl had to eat.

"Let me get my shoes."

Chapter Eighteen

Since Ander's diner didn't serve dinner on Sundays, we had to head to the next town over to find an open restaurant. The dining room was nowhere near as masculine or casual cool as Ander's, and the chef stayed hidden in the back instead of out where customers could see him. Not that it mattered—he wouldn't have the grumpy persona or bushy beard of Ander.

Basically, the place was fine...just not as good as the diner. Or maybe I'd just been hoping to see Ander that night.

Maybe.

"This is nice," Aunt Gwendolyn said, glancing around the roomful of people. "A bit noisy, but nice."

"The diner's much quieter."

"Even when full. I wonder why."

I shrugged, looking from person to person in the room. "Acoustics, maybe. Or people don't talk as loudly around Ander."

"I'll go with option number two." Aunt Gwendolyn sat back and smiled as a waiter came by with glasses of water and took our drink order. He promised to be right back, so I made sure to actually look over the dinner options. Aunt Gwendolyn must have had the same thought as she held up the overly large, plastic-covered menu. "I wonder if they have a nice salad similar to the one I like at Ander's place."

"They won't have the candied nuts if they do. Ander makes those special."

"He's quite the chef." She nodded, sneaking a sly look my way. "He's a good man, too."

Another shrug, this time one to help hide the burning sensation crawling up my neck. If I blushed, it was over. She'd never let me live that down and would likely have me married off before dessert. Not happening. "I think I'm going to have a burger."

"Not surprising, though it's a good choice. I'm sure their burgers are popular."

I sat back, looking around the restaurant again as I zeroed in on my feelings. On the static around me. I felt antsy. Something about the place, something in the air, set my nerves on edge. I just didn't know why.

"What's wrong?" Aunt Gwendolyn leaned across the table, lowering her voice. "Is it your gift? Is this too many people?"

"No, it's just..." But I had no words to explain the feeling making my heart race. Anxiety maybe, nervousness sort of. Those didn't fit right, though. It was more... "This feels wrong."

"Being in this restaurant?"

"Yeah."

She nodded. "We can go."

"No." I placed my hand over hers on the table. "We can stay—it's not the sort of wrong where I think we need to leave.

More the sort of wrong where something isn't quite right. Which makes no sense."

She smiled. "It makes all the sense in the world, dear. Are you sure you're okay staying?"

I shrugged, trying hard to stay casual. "Yeah, of course."

With a nod and a disbelieving expression, she rose to her feet, grabbing her purse along the way. "I'm going to run to the restroom. If the waiter comes back, tell him I'll have the lasagna, please. And I'd like oil and vinegar on my salad."

"Got it."

She left me alone, so I took the time to really allow myself to feel the energy of the place. It was loud, that was for sure. And crowded. But my hesitancy to relax came from more than just that. I'd been in busy restaurants before, loud ones, too. This felt different.

"Your drinks," the waiter said as he set an iced tea in front of me and a glass of wine by Aunt Gwendolyn's place. "I can come back for your orders once your companion is back."

"No need. I know what she wants." I laid out our orders—lasagna for Aunt Gwendolyn and a bacon cheeseburger for me—before examining the crowd once more.

It was as I spotted Aunt Gwendolyn moving toward the table that the reason for the wrongness in the air came to light. Or maybe leaned into the light would be a better turn of phrase.

"Everything okay?" Aunt Gwendolyn asked as she retook her seat.

I kept my eyes on the couple over her shoulder. "Apparently Joan Turlington and Corbin Lamb are besties."

She blinked at me. "They're what?"

I nodded in the direction of where the two sat at a table

halfway across the room. "Besties. Friends. They're here and having dinner together."

"They are?" Aunt Gwendolyn frowned when I indicated their position, then she dropped her napkin and leaned to pick it up, turning just enough so she could see the same two people I was looking at. Subtle, she was not, but at least she hadn't stood up and yelled their names.

When she reclaimed her seat and faced me once more, she looked confused. "How do they even know each other?"

Apparently, tonight was shrug night. "Could she be using Corbin as her Realtor for something?"

Aunt Gwendolyn shook her head. "No. She would sooner cut off her own arm than sell her house and move outside of Reverie Springs."

Quite the graphic metaphor, but I nodded along anyway. The key to her statement was the verification that Joan and Corbin didn't seem to belong together.

"I don't like this," I said. "One of the reasons I figured Corbin wasn't involved in stealing items from the manor was because he was too...not handy to deal with taking everything off and out. He's slimy enough to do it, but not the physical sort. Joan seems a little more hands-on—not super strong, but willing to put in some work."

Aunt Gwendolyn shook her head. "I just can't imagine Joan stealing from Rose or me. Or you, for that matter. She may be a little rough around the edges at times, but she doesn't strike me as a thief."

Rough around the edges *and* with a possible drinking problem. As I watched, she downed her glass of wine and signaled her waiter for another. Another night of her hitting the bottle, it seemed. Addiction of any sort could change a person's behavior to do things their friends and family hadn't thought them capable of. Was Joan struggling with alcoholism?

Our food arrived, but I was far more interested in watching the show at the other table than eating. I tried, though. Not too hard, but I at least attempted to make a dent in the food on my plate. Not a big enough one, apparently.

"Are you not liking your burger?" Aunt Gwendolyn asked, frowning.

I shook my head, still paying way too much attention to the Corbin and Joan show. Still distracted by the energy in the room. "It's okay. I don't know, it's not quite what I wanted."

She grinned and nodded, loading her fork with another bite of lasagna. "Because Ander didn't make it."

I nearly rolled my eyes. "That's ridiculous."

But not necessarily untrue. The burger was okay, just not what I had gotten used to. And wasn't that something to avoid thinking about?

"I don't like their energy," I said, refocusing on the discussion between Corbin and Joan, which had suddenly turned heated if the way Joan was using her hands to emphasize what she was saying was any sort of indication. "Something seems really off with them."

"You can't tell what, though."

"Nope. I'm too far away. But Joan seems mad—" I watched as Corbin slammed his hand down on the table and leaned closer to Joan, his face red and his expression harsh "—and Corbin doesn't look much different. What could they be arguing about?"

Aunt Gwendolyn didn't have any ideas, but I couldn't seem to stop thinking about the two. What were they doing out together in another town? What were they planning? And how could I find out?

"I think I need to go to the restroom," I said, standing up and placing my napkin on my chair. "I'll be right back."

"Be careful," she said, steeling me with a pointed look. "Don't get caught up in something that likely isn't your business."

Unless they were stealing from the manor—then it was definitely my business.

I made my way across the restaurant, doing my best to go unnoticed. Angling my path to pass the table where Corbin and Joan sat so I could maybe—just *maybe*—overhear whatever they were talking about. But as I approached, their waiter swooped in and stole their attention, ruining my shot to catch anything more than their dessert order. Or non-order. The two were calling it a night, and I had zero intel. Not how I had wanted the night to end.

I plodded to the back hallway where the restrooms were located, really disappointed in my failure to figure out Corbin and Joan's involvement with each other. Still slightly uncomfortable with the energy in the room, too. I probably spent an entire three minutes in the restroom, but it seemed like an eternity. I wanted to get back out into the dining room, to sit down and watch Corbin and Joan before they left. I needed to, so I rushed through washing my hands and yanked the door open to head back to my table. But as I walked out of the bathroom, I bumped into someone who made all the doubts disappear. Someone who calmed the energy around me.

"Ander. What are you doing here?"

He shrugged, running his hands up and down my arms where he'd caught me. "I spotted you heading in there as I came in from the back. Thought I'd wait and walk you back to your table."

His very demeanor settled something inside me, his energy

like a balm to a wound. He stopped the insistent scratching at my mind the restaurant had caused with nothing more than his presence. He was there. Strong and solid and *there*. I couldn't control my reaction.

I leaned into him and wrapped my arms around his neck, hugging him close. Letting his warmth soothe me even more.

"What's this for?" he asked even as he slipped his arms around my waist and pulled me in tighter. "Not that I'm complaining."

I chuckled and shook my head. "Complaining about me hugging you is not allowed. And this is just to say thanks for being here." I jerked back. "Wait, *why* are you here?"

"Miss Gwen called. Said you two needed some company."

Of course she had, but I couldn't be mad about it. Ander had arrived, and he was exactly what I needed to resettle myself.

"Come on," I said, untangling us but putting a hand over his where it rested on my arm so we could stay connected. "Aunt Gwendolyn's at the table. We can all have dessert together."

He followed without complaint, though I definitely heard a slight grunt when we were halfway across the room. His hand on my elbow pulled me almost to a stop, and his breath feathered across my neck as he whispered, "You know Corbin and Joan are here?"

"Yup."

Another grunt, but that was his only indication that he'd heard me. He waited until we were back at the table, where Aunt Gwendolyn had conveniently requested a third chair.

"You've been plotting," I said, nodding toward the extra chair where Ander settled.

The old woman shrugged in an exaggerated manner. "I

thought it might be nice to have some male company this evening."

"Glad I could help," Ander said as he caught the attention of the waiter. "Can I get a cup of coffee, please? Ladies, anything for you?"

"I want pie," Aunt Gwendolyn said with a smile. "Peach, with a scoop of ice cream on top."

The waiter nodded. "And for you?"

"Just a coffee, please. Decaf."

"No dessert for either of you?" Aunt Gwendolyn said once the waiter walked away.

"That burger was enough for me," I said.

Ander leaned closer. "Better than one of my burgers?"

I grinned. "Not even close."

He grunted and sat back, his legs spread and those wide shoulders taking up space. Looking toward the table where Joan and Corbin appeared to be getting ready to leave. "Any idea what Tweedledee and Tweedledum are doing here?"

"No clue," I said, eyeing Corbin as he pocketed a credit card. "Though it looks like Corbin is footing the bill."

Aunt Gwendolyn huffed. "I don't see that man as the most altruistic person in Reverie Springs."

"Altruistic, no," Ander replied. "Not an adjective I'd use for him. Opportunistic is a better descriptor."

I chuckled, smiling at the waiter as he set a coffee cup in front of me. I added sugar and cream, stirring slowly and watching the dark brew turn lighter. Sweeter. Perfect.

"How's the pie?" Ander asked, watching Aunt Gwendolyn with interest.

"Pretty good." She grabbed his spoon—which he hadn't used, as he took his coffee black—and loaded it with a good-sized bite of pie and ice cream. "Try it."

He did, accepting the bite from her without argument and chewing thoughtfully. "Not too bad. Could use some warming spices, though. A little more cinnamon, maybe some cloves. They missed an opportunity to intensify the flavors there."

Opportunity. Opportunistic. Something about hearing those two words in the same conversation struck me, and my thoughts scattered to other things that were opportunities... and that an opportunistic person would take advantage of.

"Do you think they saw us?" I asked.

Ander frowned. "Who? Joan and Corbin?"

"Yeah. Do you think they saw us here?"

He shrugged. "Maybe. Why?"

"I was just thinking that, if they were working together to steal from the manor, knowing all of us were out of town would give them the perfect opportunity to...you know. Steal from the manor."

Ander looked to Aunt Gwendolyn, who simply stared at me with a surprised expression on her face. Neither moving.

At least not until Ander jumped to his feet.

"I'll take care of the check and meet you in the parking lot."

Aunt Gwendolyn followed his lead, grabbing her purse and pushing away from the table. It was definitely time for us to go home.

Chapter Nineteen

When we arrived back at the manor—because of course Ander and Aunt Gwendolyn came with me to check on the old house—the place seemed quiet and undisturbed. At least until I actually stepped out of the car. That was when the silence of the area struck me, when I noticed the whisper of the scent of smoke on the wind. When the energy of the house came barreling in my direction.

"She's furious," I said, nearly breathless with the anger an inanimate building could have. "Something's very wrong."

Aunt Gwendolyn didn't question me, not that I expected her to, but neither did Ander. That was a surprise. He didn't know about my gift, didn't know how much I absorbed from others, including this crazy old house. He didn't know anything, but he accepted my words at face value and trusted in their truth. My respect for him leaped forward another ten notches.

"Let's go around back," he said, leading the way with a flashlight he'd brought from his truck. Prepared, the man was.

When we reached the back of the house, Elmer met us with a single tail wag as he lay on the edge of the deck with the French doors sitting wide open behind him. I cussed under my breath. "That door was locked when I left."

"And the dog was inside, I suppose?" Ander asked.

As if. "Of course."

"Someone opened the door, then. I'm assuming it wasn't our friend Elmer."

"Not possible. He's smart but too lazy to learn a skill like that."

Ander patted my smart but lazy dog—who surprisingly didn't even bother to sit up—and stayed in front of us as we headed straight for the wide-open back door. Elmer eventually fell in line, padding along behind us at a slow pace.

"No damage," Ander said as we slipped through the doorway.

I ran a finger over the jamb, agreeing with Ander. "But I changed those locks. How did they get in here?"

Aunt Gwendolyn sighed. "The manor likes to provide for its friends."

"If she's providing for a thief, then she's a stupid house."

The furnace thumped hard and loud—or what I assumed was the furnace, seeing as how the noises came from the cellar. I jumped and Ander froze, but Aunt Gwendolyn simply kept moving. Heading right for the stairs across the squeaking floorboards.

"Aunt Gwendolyn," I hissed. "Stick to the sides of the hall —these floors are so loud."

"They're not here any longer, child," she said, beckoning us to follow her. "The energy is all old."

Ander slipped in beside me, leaning down to whisper, "You feel the same energy that she does?"

"Not really. I can feel the house's anger, but not what Aunt Gwendolyn's talking about."

He nodded then hurried forward, bringing Aunt Gwendolyn to a stop at the bottom step. "How about you let me lead, Miss Gwen?"

"I can take care of myself, Ander."

"I'm fully aware of that. I'd just feel better if I took the brunt of any altercation. Just in case that old energy you feel is somehow...not so old."

She looked my way, another one of those sly smiles on her face. "I told you he was a good man."

Ever the matchmaker, that one. "Yes, I know. Ander Mendoza is a good man. Can we get on with this now?"

She nodded once then stepped aside, letting Ander—and then me—go before her. No sense in her being the one to confront a possible thief.

Ander took the opportunity to lean in and whisper to me again. "So, I'm a good man, huh?"

"Are you fishing for compliments?"

"Nope. Already reeled one in. I just want to hear it again."

"That's not happening. You get one a day. I have a feeling your ego would dominate the whole town if I gave you more."

"How do you know it doesn't already?"

Good question. "I don't, and I'm not willing to be the inciting incident of the takeover."

"Fair enough."

We reached the second floor, Ander and me pausing to look around. Aunt Gwendolyn didn't stop at all. She headed straight for the stairway to the third floor. The one behind the door I'd never been able to get through. The door that now stood open.

"Aunt Gwendolyn?"

But she was already gone, rushing up the steps in a trail of gray fabric. Looking like a ghost in the moonlight streaming in through the windows. Once on the third floor, I realized the light wasn't coming from just windows. There were skylights up there—so many skylights. At first, I thought an entire half of the roof had to be glass, but it was instead a grid of windows letting the night sky pour over us.

The room seemed...pristine. Preserved, almost. There was no five-year–thick layer of dust or look of disrepair, no falling wallpaper or water damage. This was how the room had likely been the morning of Gwen's departure, and somehow, it had remained perfect. Which was not just highly unlikely but near impossible.

The full moon above gave us plenty of light to look around, and yet Aunt Gwendolyn still turned on a small lamp. With the click of that light, the house almost seemed to sigh. To release the tension it had been holding. To go back to being at peace. The energy of the place shifted from anger to something warm and inviting. Something I hadn't felt there since I'd come to Reverie Springs. The house liked Gwendolyn being in this space.

And speaking of Aunt Gwendolyn, the woman certainly seemed to know her way around what I had to assume had been her bedroom at the manor. She moved across the floor, dragging her fingers along the bed that dominated the space. The one draped in shades of green and white with a mound of pillows at the front.

The one that had definitely been hers.

"She lived here," I whispered, watching Aunt Gwendolyn as she headed for the far side of the room. As a sense of peace wrapped around us all. As she came home.

But she obviously wasn't ready to talk about her past at the manor. Instead, she stayed as focused on the present as she could. "They're gone."

"What are gone?" Ander asked.

"The mirrors." She slowly glided to the area opposite the foot of the bed, an apparition floating across the floor, and placed her hands against the wall. "There were two large mirrors hanging here. They had been passed down through our family for generations. They were worth a lot of money..." She seemed to crumple, her shoulders sagging, her body suddenly showing its age. "Rosie had loved them."

I was beside her in a flash, wrapping myself around her as best I could. Offering comfort in a hug that would never be enough. There was so much more to Aunt Gwendolyn and especially her relationship with Rose than I knew, perhaps than I would ever know, but all that could wait. Right then, in that room under that moon, she didn't need me to know her secrets. She needed me to hold her up, to remind her that she was loved, and to do whatever I could to calm the rage inside her.

Because it *was* rage.

Much like the house when we'd arrived, Aunt Gwendolyn was livid. There was pain there, too. Heavy and dark, pulsating through her and drowning us in its negativity. But if the loss was a candle lighting the way on a dark night, the rage was a brush fire lighting up the sky and blocking out the sun. This act, this theft, had been more than the house or Aunt Gwendolyn had been prepared for. Had meant more than the others. This one had hurt...a lot.

"What can I do?" Ander asked, looking heartbroken and helpless as Aunt Gwendolyn cried in my arms. I shook my head, not knowing. Not having any idea where to start. Ander didn't argue with me or attempt to force my hand. He settled on a little club chair in the corner, one that likely would have been covered in clothes had it been in my space, and he gave us the greatest gift of all. Time and space to simply deal. He waited for Aunt Gwendolyn to stop crying, sat silently as I soothed her with words that would never come close to touching the level of pain inside her. And when she was done, when she pulled away with a soft *thank you* and once again stood on her own two feet, he rose to his and asked a different question. "What's next?"

It was Aunt Gwendolyn who answered, her energy changing to determined. Her anger a low simmer under the surface. "I want them found. Whoever has been breaking in to this house and stealing from us, I want to know their faces. I'm going to hex the stuffing out of them. Do you understand me?"

Ander nodded, a slight smile turning up the corner of his mouth. "Yes, ma'am. So should we talk strategy, or would you like a cup of tea?"

She pursed her lips, obviously thinking, before nodding once. "Tea, then strategy. Thank you, Ander."

"Don't thank me yet, Miss Gwen." He led us downstairs while I tried to figure out what was going on. Tried to come up with a plan of attack. Sadly, I had nothing.

"Does he need to be fed?" Ander asked once we reached the kitchen, the he in his question obviously Elmer...who had not followed us upstairs. My dog was even lazier than usual, it seemed.

"No. I fed him before we left. He probably needs to go out, though." I headed for the Benedict Arnold of back doors, Elmer trudging with and then past me. While he took care of his business, I stood and looked over the jamb and lockset.

There was no damage—no sign of someone kicking in the door or scratching up the metal to jimmy their way inside. Nope. The lock and jamb were pristine, which meant the intruder either had a key—unlikely since I'd changed the locks—or had picked it carefully. Or that they'd gotten inside some other way I hadn't thought of yet and had instead left through the open back door. Or...none of the above.

I sighed, my frustration building. "Seriously, this level of investigation is above my pay grade."

Elmer waddled up and huffed as if in agreement with me before slipping back inside, likely looking for a treat from the softies in the kitchen. I closed the door behind me and engaged the lock, giving the wood a good hip bump to make sure the lock held. Twisting the handle back and forth a few times for the same reason. Solid.

Maybe.

"I poured you a cup," Ander said when I entered the kitchen, sliding a heavy white mug in my direction. "It's the caffeine-free mint one you had in the cabinet."

Because being considerate was simply a trait of Ander Mendoza. "Thanks."

The three of us sat at the kitchen table, not talking. Not plotting...yet. Elmer plopped beside Aunt Gwendolyn as if he could sense that she needed his attention more than I did, even though his style of giving attention was to lay all sixty-five pounds of himself on your feet and snore. Which he did with aplomb.

"We need to find them," Aunt Gwendolyn said out of the blue, her voice quiet and rough but filled with determination. "I want them all found and brought to justice."

"We'll have to set a trap." I lifted the mug, swirling the tea as I let my mind do the same. "They came when we were out for the night—had they been watching us, or was the house being empty an opportunity they couldn't pass up?"

"We didn't tell anyone where we were going," Aunt Gwendolyn said. "It's not as if we had a plan."

I jerked my head back, ideas no longer swirling but forming solid shapes. "So let's make a plan."

Aunt Gwendolyn frowned. "I thought that was what we're doing."

"Yes, but a more public one. Let's make a public plan to be gone for an evening."

"But...where?" she asked, still not looking convinced.

"There's an all-night flea market over in Scottsborough," Ander said. "It opens Friday evening—it would take forty-five minutes just to get there and then hours of shopping time because of the size. Plus, it's at night, so we'd be away during prime breaking-in hours. Seems like a good option."

I liked his plan, but also... "There are prime breaking-in hours?"

His smile spread quick and wide. "I have to assume people who do the breaking in prefer to do it at night. When it's dark. I've never read a study or anything, though."

I really did enjoy his quick wit.

"Well, okay then. Friday. That's perfect." It was my turn to frown. "How will people know, though? The store isn't open yet, so I have no interaction with customers, and Aunt Gwendolyn wouldn't have a reason to bring up such a minor trip to anyone."

"I would," Ander said, leaning back in his chair with his mug of tea resting on his arm. "I'll have to close the restaurant to go with you two, so I'll need to make sure the whole town knows."

"Oh no," I said, shaking my head. "You can't close the restaurant."

"Why not?"

"Because...that's how you make money. I can't get in the way of your income."

He shrugged as if a full night's business—a busy night at that and one of only two dinner services he supplied each week—was nothing. "You let me worry about my income."

I was on my feet, zeroing in on that stubborn man with all the ridiculous ideas. "Fine. You worry about your income. What about your customers? They won't be happy you're closed."

Ander rose to his feet, matching every step of my own. Towering over me when we finally stood too close to move any farther. Towering...and yet not menacing. There was nothing scary about Ander to me. Maybe it was because his grumpiness was more of a front for the cinnamon roll underneath. Maybe because he treated my dog so well. Maybe because I'd seen enough of him with his customers to know he was a caring, kind man with a nurturing spirit.

Or maybe because, when we stood this close, I could finally feel the full blast of his energy. Warm, colored with attraction, and aimed directly at me.

"I won't be happy if I don't get to be involved," he said, his voice low and grumbly, his body leaning into mine as if he couldn't help it. "I'd never forgive myself if something happened to you and I wasn't there to help, so my customers will just have to deal with the fact that the restaurant is closed for one night."

He made it so hard to breathe sometimes. "And if it takes longer than one night?"

He reached out and tucked a lock of my hair behind my

ear, staring down at me with such fire in his dark eyes. "You have me for as long as you need me."

"Should I leave?"

Ander and I jumped apart at Aunt Gwendolyn's sarcastic question. The woman had also risen from her seat and ended up leaning against the wall, looking out the window and purposefully ignoring us. Or so it appeared.

"I mean," she said, lifting one shoulder, "I could leave you two alone if you needed me to."

Ander coughed. "No, ma'am. That's okay."

And it was. Okay. At least to me. There was no rush, no need to hurry anything with Ander along. I had a store to reopen, a great-aunt I'd only just met to take care of, a house that needed extensive repairs, and a thief to catch.

Speaking of which... "So, Friday. We set up a sting operation to catch a thief."

Ander's lips twitched as if holding back a smile. "Yes. Like I said, I'll let the town know since I'll need to shut down the restaurant. We can meet here—make a bit of a show of leaving together."

"But we won't be leaving," I said.

Aunt Gwendolyn nodded. "We can drive around to the barn on the edge of the property. Thomas Lee is the only one who uses it, and he won't be working late on a Friday. We'll be able to slip through the woods."

"We'll need to make sure to leave after dark," I said, knowing we'd have to run across at least a little open space to make it back inside the house. "And keep all the outside lights off. We'll also need to leave a door unlocked so we can get inside quickly."

"That can be your job," Ander said. "Miss Gwen and I can

spread the gossip. You make sure the property is good and dark."

"Sounds like a plan."

And it did. One that might just catch us a thief.

If we were lucky.

Chapter Twenty

The next few days were filled with preparations. And by preparations, I meant lies. Powered by a daily dose of Benadryl to control the inevitable breakout from fibbing so much, I spent the days telling everyone I could think of that I was going to Scottsborough for the all-night flea market and taking Aunt Gwendolyn. Most people smiled and told me to have fun, a few offered advice on how to get the best deals, while one or two showed a particular amount of interest.

The first being Corbin Lamb.

"Good morning, Corbin," I said as I stood outside the hardware store, washing down the walkway.

Corbin stepped around the wet concrete, almost glaring at my poor, sleeping Elmer. "Miss Scott. How are you doing today? Ready to open the old girl here?"

I lifted a shoulder. "Just about. Inventory is here, and the store is set. I'm just waiting on one last inspection."

"I can help you with that, you know. Make a few calls." He shot me that snake-oil smile, looking arrogant as all get-out. "I have connections with the county."

Of course he did. "I'll keep that in mind, but I think I'll just follow the normal procedure for now. Besides, I don't want to open until next week. This is my last weekend not chained to the store, and I want to take advantage of it."

"Doing something fun, then?"

Hook. Line. Sinker. I could actually *feel* the sense of excitement he seemed to be trying to hide from me. "Actually, I am. Friday, Ander, Aunt Gwendolyn, and I are heading over to Scottsborough to check out the flea market. I'm really excited about it."

He nodded, suddenly looking almost distracted. "That's a bit of a hike, and a large fair."

"I know. It runs all night—did you know that? I've never been to an all-night flea market. I'm going to be digging through booths until dawn."

Corbin did not look as if he thought that was fun. "Well, I hope you enjoy yourself. And be careful out there—coming home in the middle of the night can be a bit dangerous in these parts. Gotta watch out for the deer on the road."

Or the dogs. My stomach sank, the reminder of how Rose had died washing over me. What a thing to say. But I wasn't about to ruin our plans by calling him out on his callousness. Not today. So I pushed down any thoughts of death or loss or smacking the man upside the head.

"That's what Ander said. We may end up just staying out there—spend the day in town, you know?" And then I went in for the kill. "Aunt Gwendolyn said they have a couple of newer subdivisions out that way. Maybe I'll go look at a few houses— see what sort of thing I could get outside Reverie Springs."

That definitely caught his attention. "Why yes, there are a few new construction areas there. If you want any help negotiating with the builders, you let me know. And don't you worry about money—I'll get the manor sold. I can promise you that."

Never going to happen, but I pasted one heck of a smile on my face. "That's always an option. Well, I should get inside and finish up. You have a nice day now."

I dragged the hose around the corner of the building and took a deep breath as I waited for Elmer to follow along. The dog plodded slowly, his head down and body rolling through the motions, even wobbling a bit as he reached me.

"Did you not get enough sleep last night, buddy?"

He plopped right at my feet, grunting as if falling took effort.

Lazy dog, but still my best friend and confidant. "Elmer, I should have won an Oscar for that performance."

He growled. I liked to think it was in agreement.

Next up, more talking.

On Friday, I stood in the back of the store, waiting at the open receiving doors. Mike Allen had already rung the bell and said hello, so I knew he would be the one behind the wheel of the truck. Time to spread more lies before we left town.

"It's showtime, Elmer."

My trusty sidekick did not seem impressed. Or ready to put on a show. He didn't even seem ready to plop and snore. He'd been following me around the store—normal—but not really getting in my way—not normal. Oh well, I would need to figure out why Elmer was so morose another time. Informing Mike that we were going out of town had fallen solely on me, even though I was pretty sure he wasn't the thief. He might know the real one and happen to mention that the house would be empty so I had to sell the story. Itches or no itches.

The truck came to a stop, and I took a deep breath before plastering another fake smile on my face. *Lights. Camera. Action.*

"Hey," Mike said as he came walking through the door in his uniform. He looked happy, personable, and not at all like someone terrorizing me by breaking in to the manor and stealing things. "How's it going?"

"Good. Great. I should be opening next week."

"That's awesome news." He raised the back door of the truck and stepped into the box, squinting at the tablet in his hand. "So, you only have two bins today. Just enough to finish stocking your shelves, I suppose."

I shrugged, ready to take the green plastic containers that would be loaded with whatever little items I'd ordered. That was how being part of a wholesale co-op worked—I didn't have to buy in bulk from the manufacturer. The co-op bought in bulk, then I could buy the smaller number I needed still at a good cost. Win-win for everyone...unless your truck driver got sticky fingers with your order. Which reminded me.

"Have you ever been to the flea market in Scottsborough?"

Mike frowned a little as he set the first bin on the table so I could confirm the contents. "The all-night one?"

"Yeah. That one."

He shook his head. "Not in a long time. I used to go, though. Why? You going?"

"Yeah—Friday. Aunt Gwendolyn, Ander, and I are heading over there for dinner and some flea-market picking."

"Ander is?" He set the second box down, that frown deepening. "Who'll be cooking at the restaurant?"

"No one. He's closing it for the night."

That frown flipped, a silly sort of smile replacing it. "Oh, I see."

"What?"

"Nothing. I just hadn't realized you two were dating."

That...took me by surprise. "We're not dating."

The look on his face turned positively disbelieving. And a little smug. "He's shutting down his restaurant—his sole source of income—for the night to take you to a flea market? You're dating."

"We're really not."

"They may as well be dating," Aunt Gwendolyn said as she swept into the room from the back stairs. "Mikey, darling. How are you? How's your girlfriend doing?"

"She's good, thanks." His cheeks darkened, but he looked so ridiculously happy that the blush fit.

"Did my niece here tell you about our adventure this weekend?"

"She did," he replied. "That's why I said she and Ander were dating—he wouldn't be so ready to give up a night's income to go to a flea market with just anyone."

"True. Though, I'm going as well. Perhaps I'm the reason he's so hot to trot."

"Okay, you two," I interrupted, handing Mike back his tablet after signing for the order. Product received. Message, too. Time to get moving. "We're leaving in a couple hours, and I have a lot of work to do before then. Are we finished here?"

"Not even close," Aunt Gwendolyn said with a laugh. "Mike, dear, I brewed you something. Since I'm heading to the flea market and may find some good oils and dried plants, I figured I could use up some of what I already have." She handed Mike a small jar with a gold ribbon wrapped around the top. "This is for luck and deepening love. I hope it keeps things positive for you."

"Thanks, Miss Gwen." He looked at the bottle in his hand, frowning slightly. "Do I drink it or..."

"Goodness, no. That's what I get for being such an old lady—I forget the instructions." She took the bottle from Mike and opened it, pouring a little of the oil in her hands. "I used quality oils in here, so I recommend it as a styling product. Just apply a little bit and run your hands through your hair—it'll condition the strands and keep you from getting all frizzy even on the most humid of days."

Mike ducked so she could run the oil over his hair before standing back up. "Thanks so much. I'll definitely use it. And hey, it smells really good."

"I'm so glad you like it." She stepped back, the smile she wore looking way more satisfied than I would have expected.

Mike pulled the truck door closed and latched it, giving us one final wave before heading for the front of the truck. "You two have fun at the flea market. And thanks again for the potion."

"Bye, Mike. See you next week." I waited until he was outside, until I had the receiving door closed and locked, before turning to the smug, old woman. "You brewed him a luck potion?"

"Of course not—that wasn't a luck potion."

"Then what was it?"

"A combination of oils and plants that, when mixed properly, offer the wearer what I can only describe as a little bioluminescence."

I nearly guffawed, my eyes widening. "You put that on his hair to turn him into a human glow stick?"

"Yes." She grinned, obviously excited. "If he happens to be involved, we'll see him coming, for sure."

I wanted to laugh again, wanted to shake my head and joke about her inventiveness. She seemed excited, but I...didn't. The air had shifted suddenly, a feeling of wrongness overtaking me within a second. I tried to focus on that sense, on figuring out the cause, but to no avail. There was nothing out of place that I could tell, and I had been feeling more excited about the fake flea market trip than dreading what was to happen. Still, no matter how I thought about it, the energy felt off. I just couldn't pinpoint why.

"Did you find a way to get a message to Joan? Tell her we were going to be out of town tonight?"

Aunt Gwendolyn nodded. "Ander did. She came in for breakfast this morning, so he mentioned it. Having to close down the restaurant sure did come in handy as a way to spread the message."

It had, but I still didn't like that aspect of our plan. Didn't feel right about Ander taking on a financial burden for us. If we didn't catch the thief—if we didn't stop the person tonight—I was going to feel awfully guilty.

"I guess everything's covered, then," I said, trying hard to shake off whatever was scratching at my mind. "You're coming out to the house with Ander to pick me up?"

Aunt Gwendolyn nodded. "He's already shut down for the day. He told me he had one more thing to clean and then he'd be here to pick me up. Would you rather just drive with us? We can leave as if for Scottsborough from here, then circle around to the barn like we'd planned."

Something about that idea—about not going back to the manor—didn't sit well with me. "No. I want to go home and change."

And figure out what the heck had made me feel as if my world would soon be collapsing around me.

"You'd better get to it, then. We'll be leaving soon."

"I'm locking up now. I'll see you at the manor." And I would. Hopefully by the time she and Ander arrived, I'd have settled the unease I sensed.

Or figured out what exactly was causing it.

Worry pounded through my head all the way back to the manor. Not dread or fear of leaving, not anything to do with the flea market trip. More just...overall anxiousness. Something was wrong, and I had no idea what.

The feeling didn't leave me once I arrived home either. In fact, it seemed to intensify.

Struggling to clear my head for even a second, I unlocked the door to the manor and waited for Elmer to come inside. His steps were slower than usual, and he didn't go to his normal spot to plop. He stuck by my side instead, practically leaning into my leg.

I scratched his ears. "I really wish I could figure out what's wrong, buddy."

Elmer sighed, almost knocking me over in his effort to lay his body weight against my calf.

I finally let him go and hurried through my getting-ready-to-catch-a-thief routine. Not that I had one, mind you. I simply put on my darkest clothes and pulled my hair into a ponytail. I did apply a little makeup—I mean, I would be hanging out with Ander, and Mike did call it a date even if I disagreed—but that was about it. The whole time, though, the static I felt, the weird electric tingle, grew. Wrong, wrong, wrong. Something was very wrong.

The doorbell ringing distracted me from my worry.

"There you are," Aunt Gwendolyn said as I came downstairs. "I let myself in. I figured you wouldn't mind."

I didn't, nor did I mind that Ander had followed her inside. I'd gotten used to him being in the house at night, so there was nothing out of the ordinary with his presence. He sat on the floor with Elmer almost in his lap, the two looking like a big pile of grumpiness.

"Are you trying to bribe my dog to spend more time at the restaurant?"

Ander nodded. "Of course. He's become a little local celebrity. Though he eats me out of house and home. Don't you, big boy?"

My smile fell. Elmer had hardly eaten today. He also hadn't been outside too much. Usually, he would have scratched at the door or trotted off around the house the second we'd gotten home. Today...he'd followed me inside.

Scratchy static feeling...intensified.

"I should let him outside," I said, looking over my dog and worrying about what the universe was trying to tell me.

Sadly, the universe seemed to be far too quiet for me to hear anything specific.

"I'll do it," Ander said. He rose to his feet, patting his leg and convincing Elmer—who hunched in the middle as he rose to his feet as if the movement was a bit more than he wanted to do—to follow him down that hall and, presumably, out onto the deck. Aunt Gwendolyn stood to the side, watching me. Looking just as worried.

"What is it?"

I shook my head and started to pace, the pressure of not knowing growing inside me. Building. "I don't know, but something's wrong."

"Is the thief here?"

I shook my head again because I'd dealt with that sensation, sort of knew it. This felt different. Heavier somehow. And more confusing. I paced all the way to the back of the house, circling through the kitchen.

"I hate this," I said, my steps quickening as everything inside my gut tightened. "I can *feel* the wrongness in the air, but I don't know what it is or where it's coming from or..."

I left that last "or" hanging, but Aunt Gwendolyn didn't.

"Or at whom it's directed."

Exactly. Was this the way others felt when things started to go wrong? Did they suffer through just like me, or did they know more? Did they understand the feelings being thrown at them? I wanted to—I really did. The very idea of knowing something negative lurked nearby and there was no way to stop it felt horrible. To hear the whistle of bad news in your ear and feel the impending storm on the horizon that no one else could see was like a fire burning underneath my skin. Torture, horrible and painful and the worst feeling ever. I paced across groaning floors that grew louder with every single step, and I tried really hard to listen to the messages from the universe that she kept whispering in my ear, and I—

And then I tripped.

Not a small trip, a huge stumble where I totally lost my balance and nearly fell to the floor. I had paced to the point of speed walking through the kitchen, cutting the corners and racing past the cabinets. On that last pass, I had collided with Elmer's food bowl. The one that should have been along the wall by the French doors leading to the deck. The one I had filled myself in that very spot this morning. The contents of the bowl went flying, eggs and bits of bacon scattering across the floor. Food that should have been long gone.

My dog never let a meal go by, never left a single bite behind.

The universe—or perhaps the house herself—had just shouted at me.

"I think something's wrong with Elmer."

Chapter Twenty-One

Know how many emergency veterinarians there were in Reverie Springs? None. We had to drive to Scottsborough—home of the all-night flea market we were no longer going to—to find an office with anyone available to help my Elmer. Ander had driven as if our lives had depended on it, and maybe they had, because when I had told him I thought something was wrong with Elmer, when I'd looked into the brown eyes of the dog who'd been my best friend and had always loved me, I thought Ander's heart would break like mine was.

"Get in the van," he'd said, and we'd all listened—Aunt Gwendolyn in the front with him, me in the back with Elmer.

"Are you going to call your sister?" I'd asked, so darn worried about Elmer that I'd nearly fallen across the back seat.

Ander had simply grunted. "No. She's too far away and I don't want her to have my cell number. Now, buckle up."

Thank goodness for seat belts because the man hadn't slowed down until we had pulled up at the veterinary hospital.

But that was the only fast part about any of this. For hours, we waited as the vet and her staff ran tests and looked over Elmer. Ander had paced at first, then decided we all needed coffee and disappeared out the door to look for something better than the swill the office provided. Aunt Gwendolyn and I had continued to sit vigil—unwavering, not moving from our spots. Both of us marinating in a sense of worry and fear. There was no static to this one, no questioning anything. We were in panic mode.

I didn't need to be an empath to sense that.

Out of the blue, as we waited for the doors to the examination area to open, Aunt Gwendolyn patted my hand and sighed. "It gets better, you know."

"What does?"

"Your gift. You'll learn to control it—to block out the emotions of other people so they don't overpower your own."

Not the subject I had assumed we'd be talking about, but at least something to take my mind off...everything else. "How?"

"I'll teach you."

I sat back, sighing. "Can you feel stuff like I do?"

"No, dear. I can't." She shook her head, a small, sad little smile spreading across her face. "Your mother could, though. I started helping her to identify the emotions coming her way and to block them when she was just a child. We started with potions, little protection crystals she'd carry with her, and simple spellwork. She eventually learned to calm the gift on her own so she could live a more normal life."

One not in Reverie Springs. One without her magic. "She turned her back on her gift."

Aunt Gwendolyn went still, a feeling of something close to sadness punching through the air. "She did."

I shook my head and curled over my knees, staring at the floor. Letting the sense of right and wrong take hold so I could choose my path. So I could make the decisions I hadn't been willing to make. Until then.

"I don't want to do that."

"Do what?" Aunt Gwendolyn asked, though I had a feeling she already knew.

"I don't want to turn my back on my gift. I want to learn more about it, grow it, but figure out how to control it, because right now…"

She ran a hand over my back. "Right now, you're suffering under the weight of your own intense emotions and everyone else's on top of it. We're all worried about Elmer, and that has to be a lot for you to deal with."

I couldn't answer her, could only nod in agreement as I hugged my knees. *A lot* was an understatement—the level of worry and fear I felt, both my own and other people's, suffocated me. Leaving me with no room to breathe inside the walls of emotion surrounding me. It felt like being caught underwater—so much pressure, and all you wanted was to find the surface so you could take a breath, but there was no surface. There was no air. I had fallen too far underneath the waves, drowning in feelings.

Dying from the worry.

But there was one more thing I felt Aunt Gwendolyn needed to know.

"I'm not leaving." I sat up and shook my head, pushing past what I could. Treading water through what I couldn't. "I'm staying in Reverie Springs, I'm opening the store, and I'm fixing all the damage at Willow Manor. I'm not letting anyone run me out of town."

Aunt Gwendolyn sat silent for what felt like a long time, not saying anything, but unable or unwilling to hide her emotions from me. I felt them all—joy, relief, hope. They sprang forth, whispering through the deluge of worry. Reminding me that I was wanted and loved, even if it was by someone I hadn't known existed just a few months before. Didn't matter—we were family, and that meant something to me.

To her as well, it seemed. "Welcome home, Brylie."

Welcome home, indeed.

Ander came rushing in through the door at that moment, a cardboard tray filled with three cups of coffee in his hand. He took one look at the two of us and frowned. "Everything okay here?"

Aunt Gwendolyn chuckled softly. "Of course. We were just talking about how Brylie's going to become a permanent resident of Reverie Springs."

Ander's eyes met mine, a wave of something similar to Aunt Gwendolyn's sense of relief washing over me. He grunted his response before handing us our coffees, but he didn't need to use words to let me know how he felt about me definitely staying. I could sense it, and though Ander's emotions were harder for me to pick out, I still knew. That quiet, grumpy man with the big heart and bushy beard felt happy I would be sticking around.

So did I, to be honest.

I was just taking my second sip of coffee when the vet came out from the back, looking a little tired but with a smile on her face. That had to be good, right?

"What's wrong with Elmer?" I asked, already on my feet.

"Acute pancreatitis. I've induced vomiting, pumped him full of fluids, and we're watching for any signs of it getting worse, but so far, he looks to be stable. It was lucky you caught it—he certainly didn't exhibit any of the usual signs."

"But he'll be okay?" asked Ander, coming to stand beside

me. I grabbed hold of his arm, unable not to reach for his support. Needing some sort of connection.

The doctor, thankfully, nodded. "He should be, yes. Though I'd take a good, hard look around your property."

That one stumped me. "For what?"

"My guess would be a fertilizer," she said as she handed me a printout from her clipboard. "Here's some information on nitrogen poisoning, though he could also be reacting to an insecticide. Most likely one containing an organophosphate. Those are particularly deadly to pets."

I gripped Ander's arm tighter as I swayed a little on my feet. "Deadly?"

The vet cocked her head, looking me over. "You got him here in time. He hadn't even presented with drooling or vomiting yet, so you really saved him. But he's gotten into something in your garden."

The room turned red as those words sank in, my anger growing. "Someone poisoned my dog?"

"That's not what I said." The vet looked to Ander and Aunt Gwendolyn for support, finding none. "Elmer definitely got into something he shouldn't have—Basset hounds tend to be a bit indiscriminate about what they'll eat—but I never said it was intentional."

"You didn't have to."

Thomas Lee farmed my fields. He had promised to warn me if he was about to use anything that could hurt Elmer. He had said he would be careful. Even though I couldn't remember itching when we'd spoken, he had lied to me.

I reached out to shake the vet's hand, relieved for the moment but still furious inside. "When do I get to take him home?"

"We need to watch him for a day or two, so why don't you

give me a call tomorrow afternoon and we'll see how he's doing?"

A night—maybe two—without Elmer. Ander must have felt the way that knowledge hit me, because he edged forward, wrapping an arm around my waist as if to hold me up, and took over dealing with the doctor. Which was a good thing because my tongue had become stuck to the roof of my mouth.

"Thank you," he said, reaching to shake the doctor's hand. "We'll definitely do a sweep of the property to figure out what he got into and...eradicate it."

Those last two words held more meaning than anything else because *what he got into* was more likely *what he was fed*. And that meant he'd been targeted by someone. A person with access to fertilizers with organophosphates. Perhaps a farmer.

If Thomas Lee had poisoned my dog, I was going to kill him.

Ander tugged me closer and leaned over me, lowering his voice. "We need to go home now, Brylie."

I shuddered, because going home meant leaving Elmer behind. And that was the last thing I wanted to do. "Can I see him before I go?"

The vet nodded. "Of course. Just for a second, though—he's very weak and needs his rest."

I followed her into the back, not even looking over my shoulder at the two people left standing in the waiting room. Nothing mattered but Elmer—my partner in crime, my sidekick, and my friend. My responsibility.

The one I had failed.

"He's back here," the doctor said, opening a door that led to a room with multiple cages in it. My poor baby lay behind bars for the first time in his life, which didn't sit well with me, but I understood it. Sort of.

"He's pretty well knocked out," a younger woman said as she rose from a desk in the room. "My name's Morgan, and I'll be keeping an eye on him tonight."

I nodded, unable to open my mouth to speak. Knowing if I did, the tears would start to fall. It wasn't crying time—not yet. I had to make sure Elmer was okay, then I had to go home and figure out who had dared to do this to my dog. And then I had to destroy them.

Okay, maybe just make sure they went to jail. In my mind, though, they deserved so much more punishment than that.

Elmer lay on his side, breathing softly as he slept. Suddenly looking so small and...well, not frail. He was still my chubby puppy, but weak. Tired in a way that sleep couldn't help.

"You've got the best care," I whispered, letting one single tear fall. Giving myself that moment to crack. "I have to leave you here so they can get you better, but I'll be back tomorrow. Even if I can't bring you home yet, I'll be back to see you."

I kissed his smooth head, closing my eyes for just a moment. Elmer was more than a dog to me—he was my last link to my old life. All I had left to remind me of my dad and the hardware store in California and the life I'd lost. The dog had become my anchor, and the thought of being without him gutted me.

Jail wasn't enough for whoever did this.

"Goodnight, sweet boy." I ran my fingers over his ear, took a deep, calming breath, and turned away from the cage. "You'll call me if anything happens to him? Anything at all—doesn't matter the time."

Morgan glanced at the doctor then back at me, nodding. "Of course. Good or bad, no matter what."

"Thank you." I approached the doctor herself, holding out

my hand. "And thank you for what you did. This dog is very important to me."

"I understand. We'll take the best care of him for you."

I gave her one nod and then headed to the front, where Aunt Gwendolyn and Ander stood waiting for me.

"Everything all right?" Ander asked, his brow furrowing as he looked me over. "Are you okay?"

"She's fine," Aunt Gwendolyn said, those pale eyes locking on mine. "Angry as a hornet, but fine."

She may not have been able to sense emotions like I could, but she wasn't wrong.

"Someone did this. Someone poisoned my dog at my own home." I shook my head and grabbed what little I had brought with me, tossing my garbage in the can and striding for the door. "This ends now. We catch this person before Elmer comes home. They took things way too far."

"You'll catch them." But Aunt Gwendolyn wasn't following me out. She stood rooted to her spot, which caused me to stop in my tracks.

"We need to go," I said.

She shook her head. "I'm needed here with Elmer."

My gut clenched, and I nearly stumbled. "Do you sense something? Is he not okay?"

"He'll be fine, but my place is here with him. I'm going to stick around and perform a few chants over him." Her smile turned a little wicked. "Bring out the good side of my witch instead of playing with the bad one."

But the vet had apparently overheard her and disagreed. "There's no need for you to stay."

Aunt Gwendolyn never broke eye contact with me as she said, "Yes, there is. Don't worry, dear. I won't be in your way."

No choice, no option, no chance of refusal—Aunt

Gwendolyn was staying. I rushed to her, hugging her tight as a tiny shower of relief soothed the burn of rage within me just a little bit. Elmer would be safe with her, for sure. "Thank you."

"He's family too, you know. He's your familiar, and I won't let anyone or anything dangerous near him again." She pulled back, hanging on to my shoulders for just a moment. "Now go catch this bastard."

I glanced at Ander, finding him to be looking angry and ready for war. Feeling the power of his fury through the usual warmth of his emotions.

"We will."

Chapter Twenty-Two

I could feel the energy of the house when we pulled up behind the barn at Willow Manor. She seemed dark and lonely, heartbroken and pained in a way I had been looking past because I hadn't wanted to understand what those walls and floors and ceilings had been through. Because I'd allowed the pressure of my situation and my own baggage regarding my gift—the denial of it—to hold me back from embracing her emotions.

No more.

"I'm going in," I said as soon as Ander came to a stop. "I have to fix this."

"Fine. Let's do a quick sweep inside to make sure no one's here already here, then I'll head out to the woods as planned."

I nodded, still staring at the house, suddenly seeing her with so much more clarity.

But the house wasn't the only one I saw more clearly— Ander's emotions were suddenly right there, loud and strong and banging me over the head. His care, his concern, his...desire.

I had to tell him.

"I'm a witch," I said, my voice soft and quiet. "Like my aunt Gwendolyn, but without the smelly potions."

"So...no hexes, then."

"No. But I feel things."

"You itch when people lie."

I jerked back, my eyes darting to meet his. "How did you know that?"

He shrugged. "I pay attention." With a gentle hand, he reached for my arm, running his fingers up my wrist. "Every time someone tries to lay a line of BS on you, you start scratching. You even scratch when you're not telling the truth. It's like you're allergic to untruths."

That...was actually a really good way to explain it.

"Yeah. Basically. And I've suppressed it my entire life, but then I met Aunt Gwendolyn, and..." It was my turn to shrug.

Ander huffed a laugh. "She brought the magic out of you."

"Pretty much." I stared down at my hands, worrying my thumb along my wrist where Ander had touched me. Still wanting the feel of his warm skin against mine but scared to reach for him in case he refused. "So, are you bothered by this?"

"Bothered?"

"Does it freak you out?"

"Not in the least." Ander tipped my chin up with a finger until I was stuck staring into those dark eyes once more. "You're still Brylie to me. You've just got a little something extra going on. No harm in being extra."

I waited for an itch—for a single bit of static against my skin—but got nothing. My heart dropped then thudded fast and loud. Responding to his words, his truth, and his acceptance. Without so much as a sigh, I turned in my seat, hiking my knee up for support, and dove for him. Our lips met, our bodies crashing together as best they could over the console. He matched my desperation, tugging me in closer as he kissed me. As his hands slid a little lower to try to hang on tighter. As his tongue met mine for the briefest of moments.

Yup. That kiss would do just fine for the time being.

"Brylie," Ander said, his voice a little breathy when we parted. A little deeper than normal. "Just so you know, if we get out of this alive, I'd like to take you on a date."

I grinned. "Then I guess staying alive should be a priority."

He leaned in and kissed me again, softer this time. Sweet and gentle. The kiss of a man who simply liked kissing instead of one expecting it to lead somewhere.

"I have to go," I whispered when I finally pulled away. "We'll revisit this after."

He grunted in affirmation, keeping his forehead against mine. "There's no rush, Brylie. Let's start with the whole staying safe part. The rest will come."

And if that wasn't the best gift he could give me, I didn't know what was.

"You're a good man." I kissed him once more, a soft peck this time, then turned to hop out of the van. "Let's do this."

Ander stayed true to his word, walking me inside through the windy night and sweeping the house to make sure no one had beat us there. The rooms all sat empty, the house still and silent, so he headed outside to wait in the woods. Me? I stayed inside with the lights off, sitting in the hallway that had once been left with falling wallpaper and soaking wet wood floors. My memory played back those first few days in the house—the constant sound of dripping, the smell of mildew in the air, the feeling of grief that had enveloped me the second I'd walked through the doors. Those feelings had been so obvious, so bare to me. I hadn't seen it then, but I did now. The house had been lonely, and all I'd done was complain about it.

I had been a horrible friend to the manor.

The wind battered the side of the building, adding to the feeling of anticipation growing within me. Nearly covering up the sound of water dripping. The sound that should not have been there.

"Oh, now what?" I huffed and hurried down the hall, my nightmare coming to life again. I found a puddle just outside the powder room, though I could see no sign of where it had come from. Anger flared inside me, fueled by frustration. I had fixed this bathroom. Multiple times. I had already replaced the water lines and made sure everything was watertight. How was this leaking? And why?

I was about to throw an absolute tantrum right there in the hall when a wave of emotion washed over me. The same feeling from the day I'd first walked through the doors. I took a step back, really looking at the puddle. Silencing my mind and tucking my own emotions away as best I could to absorb what floated around me. And what floated around me was grief. The pure, heartbreaking agony of grief. I recognized it, felt it mirroring my own emotions. Knew what it felt like to miss someone so deeply that the pain never truly stopped. I gave myself a moment to truly feel what the house had been going through.

Willow Manor wasn't broken—she was crying.

"Oh, honey," I said as I ran a hand down the wall. "You've had a rough few years, haven't you?"

I took a deep breath, not fighting the feelings coming at me, breathing deep and letting the house tell me what it needed. Finding what I needed right along with it.

"It's been a rough year for me too." I slid to the floor—not caring that my foot slipped right through the puddle, not even bothered by the near-constant dripping sounds coming from somewhere close by that I already knew I would never find—and took a deep breath. "I understand how much you miss Rose because I miss my dad just the same. See, he died only a few months ago, and I haven't stopped missing him for a single second."

The sound of the house settling, the slight moan from one end, didn't surprise me, nor did it stop me from barging ahead. If talking to my grief-stricken house was wrong, I wasn't about to try to be right.

"I know your Rosie died in a car accident. My dad's death was sudden like that, too. Heart attack, though. One second, everything was great, and the next, he was gone. It's something that bites into me every single day because it took me by surprise. I'd thought my dad was healthy—getting older, but fit and not one to ignore his diet or exercise. The guilt now, the feeling of all the signs I likely missed, eats at me every single day." I took a deep breath, unbidden tears running down my cheeks, unwanted grief squeezing my heart as I said, "I can't help but wonder if he would still be alive today if only I'd have paid more attention. Which is why this thing with Elmer hit me so hard. Someone poisoned my dog, and I almost missed the signs. If I hadn't felt the wrongness, if I hadn't tripped over that bowl..."

The memory of that moment, of the food flying and the bowl being exactly where it shouldn't have been, lit up inside my mind. Truth could be a funny thing—something we didn't see until later. Something impossible to grasp or understand. Like bowls moving and creaky floors going silent and puddles forming out of nowhere. The house had always been trying to tell me things; I had simply never been open enough to listen.

That stopped tonight.

"Thank you," I said, nodding. Putting every ounce of feeling I had behind my words. "Thank you for making sure I knew there was a problem with Elmer. I promise, I'll try to listen harder from now on so you don't have to make such an effort."

The house went silent and still, the wind outside dying down as if it had stopped blowing. Even the dripping water stopped. The emotions I'd been feeling, the grief, seemed to soften. The ache stuck around, but there was a sudden softness to it. Not really a sense of healing, but close. Willow Manor and I were both dealing with losses that had gutted us. Thankfully, we both now knew we could deal with those together.

Me and the manor...besties forever.

"I should get a towel," I said, sniffling, still thinking about my dad and his constant need to fix things. His bright smile and quick wit. His comfort in dealing with people. I thought about my dad, and I knew I'd been dragging my feet opening the store because I worried I couldn't live up to his legend. He wouldn't want me to try to fill his shoes, though—he'd want me to blaze my own path. And that was what I was going to do.

So, I grabbed a towel, cleaned up the water on the floor, and I crawled back under the sink to figure out where the water had come from in the first place. No signs of leaks, no water on the lines. Everything looked to be dry as a bone.

"Okay, lady." I wiped down the base of the pedestal sink anyway, making sure to keep one hand on the wall. Making sure to give the house what she needed. Comfort. "Everything is dry here again. How about we keep it that way for a bit? I've already replaced these floors, and I really can't afford to do it again."

The temperature of the room grew quickly, the feeling one I took as her accepting my offer. At least, I hoped. Because I was really tired of cleaning up water and worrying about the floors. I could move on to other projects if I knew the plumbing was solid.

Did I mention the warmth? Because I went from comfortable to sweating like a liar in church in a matter of about a minute.

"Are you having a hot flash, old girl?" I took the towel to the laundry off the kitchen, hanging it up so that it could at least air dry until I had enough for a full load. The air grew hotter yet, making me feel as if I were in a desert. As if I'd somehow been dropped into an arid landscape and left to find my own way out.

I hadn't wanted more water, but this was ridiculous.

"Seriously, Rose. Are you trying to cook me?"

I swear, the heat turned up ten more degrees in an instant, bringing out my angry side. Making me want to rage against the house because of how uncomfortable I felt. Turning every emotion to pure, unadulterated fury.

But they weren't my emotions.

That was when it hit me—she wasn't mad at me or trying to force me out with heat. She was mad about something else. But mad was the wrong word to use. She was infuriated to the point of explosion. Willow Manor was pissed off. And I suddenly knew exactly why that was.

The thief had come back.

This time, I was ready for them. *We* were ready for them, because Ander hid just outside. I pulled out my phone—thankful to see two whole bars on the screen—and sent him a quick text, letting him know that it was showtime before heading through the family room and into the weird little vestibule leading to the front room. The shadows lay deep there, and I felt relatively safe under the archway. The position also seemed sort of middle of the house, without being too exposed like in the hallway or too trapped like in the powder room. The spot would also be easily defensible, which was just what I needed.

The snick of the back door latch releasing met my ears easily, the sounds traveling through the quiet house. Not even the wind from outside seemed to penetrate the space. Which was good, because I was able to hear the door swing open and then soft footsteps heading down the hallway, through the foyer, and up the stairs to the second floor. Creaks and groans gave away every foot placement, and I worried for about half a second that I'd never be able to follow the person without giving myself away. That half a second led to about a minute of waiting to make sure the thief was all the way upstairs—they likely wouldn't hear me from up there, right?

"Here's to hoping for some quiet floors," I whispered to no one before slipping out from under the arch and creeping through the family room. I was just about to the hallway when a shadow moved, and I had to choke back a scream. Ander stood in the kitchen, looking mean and rough and ready for battle. Grumpy chef to the rescue.

"Where?" His voice barely broke the silence of the house, but I heard him. I pointed up toward the ceiling, and he nodded, understanding me. We crept together through the foyer and to the stairs, me leading the way and hoping against hope that we wouldn't step on anything too squeaky.

And crouching, again. Seriously—why did we *do* that?

I had just placed my foot on the fifth stair tread up before I realized how silent the house had become. Not totally silent—I could hear the wind outside once more—but the floors never squeaked. The steps never released their usual creaks and groans. Every inch of the place seemed to be holding strong and solid underneath us in ways it never had before. My loud-as-heck house was dampening the sounds of our approach.

Rose's manor and I were going to get along just fine, I figured.

We made it to the second floor in total silence, and I knew. I just *knew* that this was it. I was going to catch the person who kept breaking in and stealing from Rose. I was going to find out who had poisoned my dog. Tonight was the night.

A fabric toolbox sat just outside the first bedroom—the one I'd been storing extra supplies inside. The box held a few hand tools—what looked like a hammer, some screwdrivers, my big pipe wrench. The thief had been using my tools to steal from me apparently, which seriously made me even more livid. I couldn't hold myself back. I rushed down the hall, heading straight for the door to the first bedroom, ready to confront the person.

But a figure opening the door from the third-floor staircase and stepping into the hall took me a bit by surprise. I must have surprised them, too, because once they had closed the door behind them and spotted me standing in the shadows, they froze. Staring right at me. Unknowingly trapped between Ander, who was still at the top of the stairs, and me.

Height—taller than me. Weight—more than mine. Build —bigger than me. My thief was a man. That much, I could tell, but he had his face covered, protecting his identity. For the moment.

"Put down whatever you stole and take that mask off," I said, keeping the thief's attention on me. Assuming he hadn't noticed the big man behind him just yet as he didn't seem to be reacting to Ander's presence. We had surprise on our side.

My thief stood stock still for a long second, appearing frozen in indecision, before he took a step in my direction. Fear was a funny thing, and my fear coupled with the level of aggression the thief seemed to be sending my way had my brain doing ridiculous things. Instead of standing my ground, I stumbled back and yelped, self-preservation instincts overriding my bravery for just a moment as dangerous emotions nearly overwhelmed me. As my attacker gained the upper hand.

Thankfully, I had backup. At my scream, the door to the third floor flew all the way open as if yanked, slamming straight into the thief, practically throwing him backward. Right into the arms of a charging Ander.

The rage swirling around me—both from the house and Ander—shored me up, hiding whatever the thief had been feeling behind a wall of protectiveness. I had nothing to be afraid of.

"Who do you think you are?" I hollered, grabbing a hammer from the toolbox before flicking on the overhead light. The man cringed and almost seemed to shy into Ander's body, which probably wasn't a good idea because my grumpy chef didn't look any calmer than I felt.

"I can explain," the thief said.

I recognized that voice, had heard it before. Right there in the foyer below us.

"Carl?"

Chapter Twenty-Three

I don't understand," I said, staring at the man who had been a neighbor to Willow Manor long before I had moved in. "*You're* the one who's been stealing from us?"

Carl grunted and pulled off his ski mask, not looking at me. Not answering me either. Ander tightened his grip on the older man, which seemed to remind Carl that he was caught. The neighbor deflated visibly, almost sagging in Ander's hold.

"I never stole from Miss Rose."

The fact that I didn't itch—that my gift detected no lie—infuriated me. "But you stole from my aunt Gwendolyn pretty freely."

"I had to." Carl shook his head, wincing. "Could you let me go, Ander? I promise not to do anything wrong."

"Nope," Ander said, popping that P and hanging on to Carl with a strong hold.

I snorted, refocusing on the old man in Ander's custody. "Won't do anything wrong? Like break in to a house that isn't yours and take things you don't own? Like scare the living daylights out of people supposed to be living in that house?" I stalked closer, my anger growing with every step. "Like poisoning your neighbor's dog?"

"Whoa," Carl said, putting his hands up. "I never poisoned no dog. I may not have been the best neighbor to you, but I certainly didn't go that far."

No itching—no lies. I had no idea how that was possible. I had been certain the thief had been the one to poison Elmer, but maybe I'd been wrong.

"Let him go, Ander," I said, watching warily as my mind spun with this new knowledge.

Ander huffed as he let the old man go, staying close but no longer controlling him. "And by the way, no one *has* to steal."

"I did." Carl stretched his neck, looking slightly pained. Good. After all the cricks in my back from sleeping in my minivan because he made me feel unsafe in my own house, he deserved a little ache.

"So, you just...made yourself at home. Here." I shook my head, trying hard to balance the anger and the confusion still swirling around me. "I just don't get it. You steal all this stuff from your neighbor, and...what? Hope we never pop over and notice our mantel or cabinet hardware or mirrors in your house?"

"I never used the stuff myself, and I wasn't planning on sticking around." He sighed and leaned his back against the wall. "I'm not a bad guy, you know."

Ander grunted, but I shot him a look to quiet him.

"I never said you were a bad guy—I said you were a thief."

"If you got everything stolen from you, you'd have to make choices you wouldn't normally make, too." He sagged a little more. "I loved Miss Rose—she was a great person who would have given anyone the shirt off her back. I never would have done anything to hurt her. But she'd died, the house sat empty, and I needed money. If she'd been alive, she would have helped me, so I figured…"

"You figured it was okay to take what she wasn't using as a form of her helping you."

"Yeah." He sighed again, rubbing his neck. "When the mill went under, they took my pension with them. I figured I could sell my house and get a little money out of it, but Corbin Lamb said he couldn't sell it in the shape it was in. I didn't have the funds to fix it, but I didn't have the option not to either. And no one lived here. I just figured the stuff was better off being used than being left out here to rot."

Because that was what Aunt Gwendolyn had allowed to happen—she'd walked away from her home and left it to decompose right there in the sun. But that didn't excuse his actions, especially not since I'd come to town.

"You should have stopped once I moved in. You knew someone was living here, and you kept stealing."

"I was this close to finishing the repairs. Just a couple more thousand, and I would have been out of your hair for good."

Still no lies detected, not that it mattered. A thief was a thief was a thief. Good reasons or bad, he still took what wasn't his.

"You scared me."

Carl stared at the floor. "I just wanted you to leave so I could finish what I started and get the hell out of Reverie Springs. That was all."

It was my turn to shake my head, my turn to mull over what Carl had done and how it had affected me. I'd thought I was going insane. I'd been thinking about leaving the only family I had left. I slept in a *minivan* for a month.

"I refuse to feel sorry for you," I said.

Ander gave me a pointed stare, the kind that asked a

question. The kind that said *what do you want to do?* Thankfully, I didn't have to think too hard about it.

"While I can appreciate the why behind you stealing from us, I can't let it go." I took my phone out of my pocket, swiping it to life and tapping out the three little numbers the situation required. "How did you get in here, by the way?"

"There's an unlocked window in the conservatory. I crawled through."

"And then opened the door from the inside."

"Yeah. I'm too old to be crawling through windows when I don't have to."

I shook my head and huffed. Of all the stupid... I'd changed all the locks in the house but hadn't even bothered to check the conservatory windows. Lesson learned.

"Well, thank you for that. I appreciate your honesty."

Carl looked up, something too close to hope in his eyes. "Does that mean you won't be calling in the sheriff?"

"Nope." I finished dialing, putting the phone on speaker so he could hear every word between us. "Rose's home deserves better than to be used as a junkyard."

An hour after the sheriff left with Carl in handcuffs, I walked into the vet's office in Scottsborough. The girl behind the desk smiled and waved me into the back where I'd said goodbye to Elmer just a few hours before. I found Aunt Gwendolyn in the room with the cages, her lips moving slightly as she whispered what sounded like chants to the sleeping Basset hound in her lap. She glanced up at me, smiling softly.

"Everything good?"

I nodded as I knelt beside her. "It was Carl."

She hummed, not looking surprised. I was by her reaction, though.

"You knew?"

"No," she said, running a hand over Elmer's neck when he groaned in his sleep. "I never would have thought he was capable of stealing from my Rose, but people seem to surprise me more and more lately."

Her Rose. The thief had been taking from Rose in Gwendolyn's mind, not from her. The pieces of the puzzle of Rose and Gwendolyn and the manor began to slide into place. The emotions of the house, the sadness following Aunt Gwendolyn around, the third-floor bedroom where she felt so comfortable, Joan's ire. I was an idiot who should have seen what was right in front of my face.

I saw now, though. "She wasn't just your friend, was she?"

Aunt Gwendolyn didn't look up, didn't meet my gaze. She kept her eyes firmly planted on Elmer as she continued to stroke his fur. "No, she wasn't *just* my friend."

But she didn't say anything more. I could sense the worry within her, the anxiety. As if there was something she needed to say but was afraid to. As if she feared her admission might make me see her a different way.

Ludicrous.

"You don't have to hide with me," I said, reaching out to still her hand. "You can trust me."

But her nerves didn't ebb; her worry didn't fade. And while I felt as if she should feel safe telling me something so personal, I also understood that sometimes secrets were harder to let go of than we'd want for them to be.

"Sorry," I said, shaking my head. "I don't mean to push

you. You can tell me or not, it won't change anything between us. Our relationship can grow on your timeline. I promise."

Aunt Gwendolyn took a deep breath, tears welling in her eyes as they met mine. "You are such a gift, Brylie. Not just to me, but to everyone."

I squeezed her hand tighter, not looking away. "I don't always feel like it, but I'm glad you think of me as one."

"I do, and Rose would have as well. She would have loved you, for sure." She sighed and went back to running a hand over Elmer's fur. "Rose was far more than a friend or business partner to me, as you've already guessed. She was my life partner—I considered her my wife, even though, back when we fell in love, we weren't allowed to be married."

"That's why all the gray."

She frowned. "Pardon?"

"The gray. You never wear any colors—just black, gray, and silver. They're your mourning clothes."

She huffed a sad little sound that nearly broke my heart. "I suppose they are. I hadn't really thought about it, but you're right. I've avoided bright colors since her death."

"You would look amazing in green." I sighed, needing to ask a question I was pretty sure I knew the answer to. Remembering how Joan had told Aunt Gwendolyn she'd "always been wrong" and now knowing why those words had seemed to hit the older woman so hard. Needing to understand the whole situation so I knew how to deal with the people around us. "So...I hate to ask, but were you two...out?"

"Oh, goodness no. We kept everything quiet, though I have a feeling there were plenty of people who knew and simply chose not to comment. Some knew and chose *to* comment, but we ignored them for the most part. Rose's family definitely didn't like us together, but she never wavered when faced with their ignorance."

"Joan."

"Yes, Joan. That's why Rose didn't leave her sister anything in her will. That woman never could accept us."

"Well, she's an idiot, then."

Aunt Gwendolyn chuckled. "Perhaps she is, but Rosie still loved her. She was able to look beyond her sister's ignorance most of the time. She occasionally lost her temper and called her sister an ignorant nincompoop just to irritate her, though."

Ignorant nincompoop. I liked it. "Rose sounds amazing and strong."

"She was." Her voice cracked, and those tears she'd been holding back fell hard and fast. "We were together for fifty years before that night on the highway. I can barely remember a time before her, and I don't know how to be me without her by my side."

A wave of emotion washed over me, years of pent-up hurt and pain swallowing me whole. My poor aunt had been dealing with the loss of her beloved wife for years without the sort of public support she'd have gotten if Rose had been Roger instead. That was inexcusable to me.

I rose onto my knees and grabbed her, hugging her close as she cried. Trying like crazy to absorb some of her hurt, to take the weight of her grief from her shoulders. To bear it for her. And finally—*finally*—understanding the emotions of the manor itself. "She misses you, too."

Aunt Gwendolyn sat back, wiping her face. "You see her spirit?"

"No, but she's there in the house. I hear her sometimes, feel the grief around me. I didn't recognize it at first, but that's what it is. Beyond the house itself, Rose is still in those walls.

Her energy. She misses you. Her love is palpable and has become part of the house you shared."

She nodded sadly, almost disappointed, it seemed. "I'd hoped she'd be there but didn't want her to be at the same time. I wouldn't want her stuck between worlds."

"I don't think she is. I think your love infused the very spirit of the house, and that's what I feel. The echo of the emotions. The shadow from how strong they were."

Aunt Gwendolyn's lips turned up in a soft, sad sort of smile. "They were definitely strong. All fifty years were amazing, even though we had to hide our relationship." She sniffed and took a deep breath. "At least her energy is still here on earth with me."

"It is. The house loves you and wants you to be happy. It wants your energy around it."

She looked up as I gripped her hand, my eyes trying to tell her the things I needed to. That she was loved, appreciated... and welcomed.

Thankfully, she seemed to understand my wordless pleas. "Well then, perhaps it's time for me to come home. If you don't think you'd mind the company."

I pursed my lips, pretending to think it over, before grinning her way. "I don't mind. But no brewing hexes in the house."

She laughed. "Don't worry, Brylie. Rose used to have the same rule—that's why there's a workshop in the garage."

"She sent you all the way out there?"

"Child, she had the thing *built* for me and my potion brewing. She hated hexing days."

I had a feeling Rose and I would have gotten along just fine. "Then we'll revitalize it for you and get you set up for more brewing. Not in the house."

Elmer chose that moment to yawn and stretch, groaning loudly as if we had woken him.

"Are we disturbing your beauty sleep?" I asked, patting his head. He stretched his neck and pressed his cold, wet nose against my palm as Aunt Gwendolyn rested her fingers along the back of my hand, the three of us interconnected. Family...reunited.

Chapter Twenty-Four

The day that I was to turn the hardware store's sign to open for the first time was a cold and rainy Friday, but I knew the people of Reverie Springs would show up anyway. I would forever be grateful for their interest in my business. As would be my wallet. Making money again would be a good thing.

As I rolled into town to get ready for my big day, I thought back over how far I'd come just in the past few weeks. The store was ready, the shelves were stocked, a picture of my dad hung near the cash registers, and a big bed for Elmer lay behind the service desk. But the store wasn't the only thing that was ready for new adventures.

Aunt Gwendolyn had moved in to the manor as expected. She'd argued with me about what room to take, but I'd eventually won, moving her in to the suite on the top floor. It didn't feel right to take the room she'd shared with Rose, so Elmer and I bunked in one of the suites on the second floor. Ander went back to sleeping at his own place, though he did spend a lot of time at the manor. Seemed he really liked cooking in our big kitchen even though it needed a major makeover. He may have liked the company, too.

Carl had pled guilty to the breaking and entering and theft charges brought against him. The DA had offered him a plea deal to keep him out of jail if he returned what he could, and the old man had taken it. All for the best, really. He'd done bad things for what he felt were good reasons. Deep down, I wasn't sure if I could blame him. He was wrong, but would I do something similar if I had to? I couldn't say definitively, so I'd agreed with the plea deal. Plus, having his crimes broadcast around to all the people who'd known him for decades seemed punishment enough in a lot of ways, especially after he brought back the cabinet hardware, the picture of Rose's great-great-great-grandfather that had hung in the powder room, and the mirrors from the third-floor bedroom. Aunt Gwendolyn had nearly cried when she'd seen them, and my heart had melted. That was all she'd wanted—her mementos back where they belonged.

Sometimes justice wasn't about penance.

But I'd stopped using the powder room completely—the picture was creepy, and I felt as if I were being watched in there. No thanks, Rose.

Elmer made a full recovery, though he went through a phase where he refused to go anywhere without me. I didn't blame him—I went through the same phase, practically panicking if he left my sight. There was no evidence that anyone had intentionally poisoned him, but I still worried. Thomas Lee had invited me into his barn to look at all his available chemicals, and while we hadn't found any containing organophosphates, we still removed the ones that might be a danger to a pet. I had also decided our routine had to be adjusted for Elmer's safety. I walked my chubby sidekick around the backyard every morning, and Aunt Gwendolyn made sure he got more exercise in the afternoon while I worked. And Ander...well, he spoiled my dog.

And me.

And Aunt Gwendolyn.

That grumpy chef wasn't as grumpy as I'd thought. He also was a man of his word—he'd asked me out on a date as soon as the charges against Carl had been announced. In fact, he'd asked me out on many, many dates in the following weeks. I was officially dating the owner of the diner next door to my hardware store, a fact that made me awfully happy.

"Hey," he said with a smile when I walked into the diner that grand-opening morning. "Eggs and toast?"

I grinned—the man knew me. "Yes, please."

He hurried over to kiss my cheek, then sauntered back behind the flat top and started making my breakfast. I noticed the ground turkey with an egg in it next to my order—that would be for Elmer. Ander was convinced that prepared kibble was part of what had made him so sick, so he cooked every meal for my dog. See? Spoiled.

I still hadn't gotten the whole story behind the landline phone and why it was the only number his sister could have, but I didn't push the man for answers. All would come in good time. And if not what I deemed as soon enough, well...fine. It would drive me crazy. He would tell me eventually, and I would have to accept the wait.

Patience had never been one of my virtues, but I would try.

As I contemplated difficult family relationships and future plans, the bell over the door dinged. I glanced up just in time to see Corbin Lamb strolling inside. I nearly groaned—the man had been to see me way too many times over the past few weeks, always trolling for business. Always pushing me to sell the manor. That wasn't going to happen, but he didn't know how to take no for an answer.

"Brylie," he said, giving me that signature snake-oil smile. "How's my favorite new resident doing?"

"I'm good, thanks. How's the real estate market?"

"Good. Good. It's a great time to sell."

A loud clang from the kitchen area almost made me grin. Ander was paying attention, which was fine. He knew I wasn't going anywhere.

"That's great. By the way, you should stop by the store this weekend. We've got some great grand opening sales running, and Aunt Gwendolyn has some new potions she brewed for luck."

His chuckle sounded strained. "Ah, of course. Miss Gwen's famous potions. So, no more hexing?"

"Oh no, she's still hexing." My smile widened as his eyes went round. "But only when people deserve it. You haven't caused her vexation lately, have you?"

"No. Of course not." He took a step back, hands up at shoulder level. "I've been so busy with work, I haven't had time to be out much."

"Really? I could have sworn I saw you out with Joan Turlington not too long ago."

He scoffed. "Me? No. What would I have to do with Joan?"

My elbow itched, the lies he told obvious...to me. Funny. The man may not have been the thief I'd been chasing, but he definitely had secrets. As did I. As did just about everyone in this town. Didn't matter that he didn't want me to know something. I'd figure it out eventually. That was the thing about small towns—everyone ended up knowing your business. Especially the witchy empath next door. I didn't mind, though. My business was hardware, hexes, and handsome chefs. All things I didn't need to keep hidden from others in town. So as I sat down to eat my breakfast, as I looked out the window at the treelined Main Street just coming to life, I grinned and grabbed a pen to write myself a message.

Welcome to Reverie Springs—don't mind the hexes.

Acknowledgments

As Ellis Leigh & Kristin Harte, I've written close to fifty novels. That's a lot of words, and my poor editor Lisa Hollett has had to read them all. I was thrilled that she once again allowed me to rely on her skills to polish my mystery manuscript. I couldn't write without her.

During the pandemic, a group of authors and I met every Thursday night on Zoom to chat, talk shop, and try to deal with the stress of writing happiness while the world burned around us. To Zoe, Selena, Brighton, Molly, Annika, and the occasional guest stars—thank you. I wish nothing but success for all of you.

To my Bitches™. There are no words to thank you for the daily love our group exudes. Thank you Suz & Esher for reading this adventure in the early days—I always appreciate your guidance. Bitches do bail.

To my family, especially my two babies. I finally wrote a book you can read!

Millie Thorne is the not-so-secret pen name of a USA Today bestselling romance author who wanted a little more magic and mystery in her work. She started writing the Brylie Scott Mystery Series after the image of a house crying popped into her head and refused to leave. If Rose Manor had any sort of manners, it would be paying rent after all these years. Millie lives in the Midwest with a family of miscreants and a dog that makes a wonderful doorstop.

For all the latest on Reverie Springs gossip and updates, subscribe to Millie's newsletter.

www.milliethorne.com/news